Would You Believe Love?

Would You Believe Love?

by Eliza McCormack

Random House New York

Published in the United States by Random House, Inc., New York, and simultaneously in Canada by Random House of Canada Limited, Toronto.

ISBN: 0-394-47298-5
Library of Congress Catalog Card Number: 78-162956

Manufactured in the United States of America

98765432

First Edition

For
Mother and Father
and
Minnie

Would You Believe Love?

Thursday, Sept. 18

Therapist Day and Ass Bird off on sex again. It's a legitimate topic but the way AB goes at it sets my teeth on edge. He makes me feel like the 98-lb. weakling receiving instructions from Charles Atlas on how to build up my biceps.

He starts off by asking if I have had any sex. If I say yes, he wants to know how often and how it was. If the answer is no, he asks if I've been masturbating. I've told him and told him that I don't masturbate but he doesn't believe me and always acts as if this time he will catch me with my metaphorical pants down and get the truth.

Today, when I said J. and I hadn't had interc. in the past week (because I had avoided it), AB gave me a long pep talk on the male ego and sex drives and told me I must make more of an effort to be receptive and to satisfy my husband. He said I should read "suggestive" books before bed and said he had had good reports of a paperback called "My Secret Life."

I dutifully wrote down the title but I thought how

Ass-Bird-Backwards this "therapeutic" reading is. I've read sex manuals, some suggested by AB, but they don't do any good. And why should anybody think they would? It's what goes on between two people *before* they go to bed that determines how good or bad the sex will be.

As I put the slip of paper in my purse, I suddenly had a vision of AB's other patients with their little slips of paper all turning up in droves at the bookstore, all asking for "My Secret Life." And I laughed and said, You could become the Pornography King-Maker of Cambridge, Mass. You might even get a rake-off from the publishers.

AB said icily that I would do better to address myself to my problems than to make childish jokes and that this book is therapy, not pornography. And I realized I had said the wrong thing. It begins to seem that I can never say anything but the wrong thing. I left his office, feeling as I so often do, that I am the wrong person in the wrong place at the wrong time. I keep feeling that I don't fit anywhere . . . not in AB's therapy, not at home, not with J. (in or out of bed), not even with my children anymore.

To Harvard Square and bought the book and then I wandered around awhile. The Hare Krishna kids were making a Joyful Noise in front of the kiosk and as I dropped some money into their basket, I felt like saying, Pray for me in my hour of need.

For I am in need. I feel cut off from everybody, like a deep sea diver in a heavy suit viewing the world from behind a little glass window.

Finally I went home and J. was already here. He

was standing at the fridge with his back to me and I had the oddest sensation that this was some stranger who'd wandered into the wrong house. Who he? I thought, looking at the tall spare figure in the gray flannel suit with the gray flannel hair on his gray flannel head.

Then he turned and I saw his face . . . his so American face . . . a combination of The Wall St. Journal and The Farmer's Almanac and I knew I had met him someplace but it did not seem possible that he is the man to whom I have been married these many years and with whom I have had 2 now nearly-grown children.

I gave him what I meant to be a friendly greeting and asked how he'd got back from D.C. so soon.

He said an Administration official had given them The Word on some poverty programs and The Word had been so depressing the meeting never got off the ground and they had quit early.

I said I didn't understand why, since he so disapproves of this Administration, he serves it in any way at all.

He bristled and said he does *not* serve it; that he works with groups outside the government that are trying to keep things from collapsing. Then, screwing the top on the vermouth bottle as if he were wringing its neck, he said, All your civil-rights battles won't help much if there are no jobs. And if this recession continues, there will be no jobs. At least not for your soul brothers. Then, with an air of having dealt with a particularly moronic question, he left the kitchen.

Am I becoming paranoid? Or is it a fact that J. doesn't like me? Maybe he loves me in some kind of way (probably the way Old Dog Tray's master loved ODT) but I don't think he likes me. And I must admit that sometimes I don't like him very much. In fact, sometimes I actively dislike him. And all Economists. They think they know everything about everything when most of them don't know very much about anything except Economics and often they are wrong about that. Why didn't I marry some kind of scientist, like maybe a physicist who would keep his nose on a laser beam? No, perish the thought. The physicists we know are always spouting off and always on committees. I guess other people's husbands just look greener.

As I was getting dinner, Ames came in looking, I thought, more friendly than usual. Most days she goes around like The Girl in the Iron Mask. It's amazing how forbidding such a beautiful girl can look. And she is beautiful, with her blue eyes (like J.'s) and her corn-silky hair which she is always trying to get the curl out of and, once upon a time, she had a smile that would light up a blacked-out city.

She kept dipping into the Apple Crisp and I stupidly made the mistake of saying she would spoil her appetite. (Will I never learn not to speak unless spoken to?) Instantly, she dropped the spoon, put on the Iron Mask and left the kitchen without a word.

I stood there feeling as if a door had been slammed shut in my face. Then I reminded myself that I am always overreacting (as J. says), that 16 is an age of disequilibrium (as AB says) and that Ames doesn't really hate me, she just acts like it sometimes. I resolved that dinner would be cheerful and that I would be as relaxed as the old shoe which I very much resemble these days.

The meal began amiably. I read aloud a letter from David. He's only been at this school a short time but already he has criticisms of everything: his teachers, the courses, the sports, the food. I see (he wrote) lots of room for improvement but I think something can be done.

We laughed but I was appalled at how pompous my 14-year-old son is sounding. Where is the beautiful barefoot boy of last summer?

Then J. called Ames "Meg." She renounced Meg a year ago, saying she wanted to be called by her middle name, but J. keeps forgetting and this infuriates her. This time it ended our little family feast as Ames rose, looked coldly down on us and said, I've had enough.

Later, I got to thinking about Ass Bird. I feel guilty about spending all this money on him. And to no point. Yet, somehow, I'm afraid to quit. My mind turned this way and that, like a rat in a maze, trying to decide what to do. Finally, I went in to ask J. what he thinks.

He was at his desk, surrounded by the usual mountain of paper, with a sheet of figures in front of him. I apologized for interrupting and said I'd like to talk to him when he came to a stopping place.

He said there wasn't any stopping place. Then, with a smile but with his finger still on the figures, he asked, What's on your mind?

When J.'s at his desk there is no way to face him except standing backed up against the wall so that is where I stood. I said I thought I was wasting my time and his money with Ass Bird because my depression was as black as ever.

J. said perhaps I should try somebody else and I answered that I hadn't the strength to start all over.

His eyes wandered back to the figures and I said hurriedly. Could we make an appointment to talk?

I'd be glad to talk, he said, but I don't know what to say. I'd hoped you were being helped but if you aren't . . . Still, you shouldn't quit therapy. You should have somebody.

His words seemed to resound in the room . . . you should have somebody. And it seemed to me the answer was equally resounding: Aren't *you* somebody? Can't you help me?

But I didn't say anything and after a moment he looked down at the figures and said, Why don't you try a little longer with this man?

I looked at his bent head and opened my mouth to say something. Then, as I saw him pick up the pencil, I clamped my jaws shut and left the room. I felt as if I had been standing on a street corner holding out my tin cup and J. had walked right on by me.

I suppose, according to J.'s lights, there isn't anything he can do. But J.'s lights are pretty dim. Couldn't he at least say something? Anything that would not leave me wandering lonely as a big, black rain cloud.

AB says my loneliness is inside me (where the hell else would it be?), that a person with a devoted husband, two children and twice as many friends as most people cannot, in fact, be lonely. I don't think AB knows my head from a hole in the ground.

When I went upstairs I saw "My Secret Life" on the table and I left it there, knowing there wasn't a prayer it could make me more receptive to J. tonight.

Now I'm going to bed and read the great biography of Lytton Strachey. I know why Carrington loved him so much. He TALKED.

Saturday, Sept. 20

With Deb to the hairdresser yesterday because she keeps telling me it'll bolster my spirits. I complained to the man about all the gray in my hair. He said it is not gray but a beautiful white gold mixed in with the yellow gold, and not to let anybody fool with it. That did a lot more for me than any of AB's expensive attentions.

Last night at dinner Ames told us she wants to quit school. She said nothing in school means anything and I ventured that things outside school mean a lot less. J. said not to listen to me and he launched into a peroration about preparing oneself and the joys of the mind and the rest of the Pilgrim Ethic or whatever the hell it is he lives by.

Later, as she and I stacked the dishwasher, I tried to find out if there is any particular reason why she wants to leave school. She had a few minor criticisms but nothing much. She also had no idea of what she would do if she left school. This made me think she doesn't want to leave school so much as she wants something to happen there. I made a mental note to call and get an appointment with her adviser. Maybe I can find out something from him.

J. in D.C. again and won't be back until late tonight. It is becoming almost a relief to have him away. When he is not here I cannot expect anything from him and so I am never disappointed.

Sunday, Sept. 21

Gloomy day.

J. home late last night; up early this a.m. and wouldn't take time to eat breakfast, just took his coffee into his study. Said he had to work on his lectures and he was not at home to anybody. Not to me either, apparently.

I started the Xword but suddenly could not stand this empty, lifeless house so went for a walk. Stopped in at Deb's to find her worried and furious at Marsden, who hasn't paid Kathy's tuition (which had been part of the divorce agreement).

After some argument with him, Deb discovered that Molly (Marsden's new wife) is pregnant, they have bought a house and Marsden considers himself too burdened to pay for the private school.

After we had jumped up and down on Marsden for a while I told Deb I would lend her the first quarter's tuition (which my secret savings account will just about cover) and that Marsden will eventually find the money.

Tried to get her to come out and have a sandwich with me but she had got going on the sherry and finally I had to leave her to it.

Came home feeling even more depressed and thought of taking one of those anti-depressant pills AB gave me. Decided it is less bad for all of me to feel awful than for me to split in two (as I do with those pills). Then one of me feels awful while the other one wrings its hands over the awful one. Some time ago I described this feeling to AB and he told me such a reaction has never been observed with these pills; as much as to say I am not entitled to have it.

When I looked in on J. in the afternoon, he was sitting there with the lights on, the curtains still closed. He was so deep in what he was doing that he did not notice that I came in, opened the curtains and turned off the lights.

I asked when he'd like dinner and he said could I just bring him a sandwich; that he had too much to do to stop.

It is now 10:30 and he has been immured in there for over twelve hours. I would like to say this is no way to live but the eternal question is, who listens?

Some time ago I told AB, jokingly, of course, that the solution to all my problems would be to run off to Mexico and find myself a lover. Now I am thinking, and not jokingly, to hell with the lover. I just want to run away. Somewhere out there the sun must be shining and people must be talking, even laughing, and I want to run away to wherever they are.

Wednesday, Sept. 24

AB at me again about getting a job; said I would be much more cheerful if I would do something with people. Reminded him I still teach swimming at the Blind School. Oh, but that's children and a part of my good-works syndrome. I said children are people and the teaching is work even though I am not paid.

He brushed that aside, saying I should get a REAL job. I told him there aren't any real jobs for a middle-aged white woman with nothing but an old bachelor's degree (and in Philosophy, of all useless subjects) and I started to tell him about what I've seen in the want ads.

But, looking at me sternly through his great big glasses, he said if I really wanted a job I could get one.

And of course he is right. If I had to support my children, I would sell stockings or wait on tables or go from door to door with encyclopedias. But, lacking that necessity, I would as soon put my head in the oven as do any of the jobs that are open to people like me.

Telephoned my dear, good sister tonight. Whenever I count my blessings (all 2 or 3 of them) I put Cissy high on the list.

She asked about me and I told her things are fine but sometimes I get a little (what a laugh) lonely; that J. is so busy saving the world he hardly knows his own name, let alone mine.

She said her problem is just the reverse: Alex hangs around all the time, cooking organic food and bringing home hippie types to eat it. She wishes he would clear out and get back to the store. Which (she said) badly needs his attention. He has a bunch of bearded weirdos in there (she said) and I am worried that instead of it being THE scholarly bookstore, it will become THE psychedelic center.

The news of "little" Sophie (she's 20 now) is that she's supposed to be at Berkeley but she is busy trying to make a revolution.

I am (Cissy said) getting sick of revolt, revolution, youth and yogurt.

Then she said I should come out for a couple of weeks and we would sit up all night talking about everything. I said I would try but I know I won't make it.

I've tried to get to S.F. for years now and something always comes up.

At the end she said to remember if I could get through the next five or six years, I'd be all right. Nothing much matters after that, she said.

After I hung up I almost cried. It's bad when things matter too much but I wouldn't want to live if they didn't matter at all.

Thursday, Sept. 25

Tonight I tried AB's pornographic prescription.

J. and I had been to a dinner at the Academy and coming home we had words about whether it was dull or not (my position being that it was) so it was not the most propitious time to try a sex reclamation project. But we might both be in our graves if I wait for a propitious time.

When we got home, J. went to his study. I went up, bathed, got into bed and settled myself to get into "My Secret Life."

It took some doing. There were six prefaces; one by G. Legman (surely a joke?) was over forty pages. Finally came to what could be called the meat of it. The first chapter of childhood recollections, watching girls urinate and messing around with his penis, discouraged me but I made myself keep on.

At last there was a chapter headed, among other things, My First Fuck. Figuring this must be what the doctor ordered, I read and waited for feelings of sexual arousal.

But it was the old seduction of the housemaid; the hero stalking her for days, upstairs and downstairs and in and out of the house. Finally cornering her, he screwed her as she lay half-fainting, begging him (as he said) to desist.

It aroused me, all right. But not sexually. I was angry at the hero and his view of life (no broader than the space between a woman's legs); at the Victorians and their small, smelly minds; at AB for thinking I would find this exciting and at all men whose interest in women is confined to the "cunt," the "hole," and "the red-lipped, hairy thing between their legs."

Finally I realized that if I kept on reading, it was liable to put me off sex for life and I dropped it. Took up Lytton and read that awhile and gradually calmed down and then got sleepy and turned out the light.

I was not quite asleep when I heard a car stop outside. It stayed there a minute, with the motor running, then the car door slammed and it drove off. I lay there, looking at the shadows of the trees on the wall opposite the bed, trying to think what the car . . . and the shadows, too a little . . . reminded me of.

It was a French movie I saw not long ago, about a man and woman who met by chance. He was a hitch-hiker and she picked him up (the car sounded like the one outside the window). They went to her house which was way out in the country and they spent half the night wandering through a field together. The moon shone and the trees were shadowy against the sky.

By the time they went back to the house and went to bed I was crying (I was alone so I could cry all I wanted). The intercourse was lovely, though you never saw anything but their faces and their hands. He held her hand the whole time.

And as I thought of them walking together and sleeping together and holding hands, I realized again that no matter what AB says, I am lonely.

I must've been almost asleep when J. came to bed. But when he laid his heavy hand on me, I awoke completely and I sat up and said, Jesus Christ!

All the anger I felt at the cunt-crazy hero came back and I said, What do you think I am? Just a hole?

Then J. turned over, pulled the covers up and never said another word.

I crept out and came to the guest room but I couldn't sleep here either. It was too late to take a sleeping pill (and I feel guilty about taking them anyway) so I went down and had some Sanka. Now I am feeling ashamed of myself. It was not J.'s fault that Ass Bird's pornography backfired and I should not have vented my anger on him. I also don't like what I said. But he shouldn't have accepted it. He should have made some answer. He should have SAID something.

I wish now I had stayed and had told him about the book. Maybe then he would've said something. Maybe we would even have laughed about it.

Friday, Sept. 26

Felt so absolutely out of it, off by myself in a cold, gray world, that I knew I had to get out of the house or I'd burn it down with me in it.

Made up some bags of old clothes and took them to the clothing collection center. On the way, saw a sign above the door of a basement saying "Draft Counseling." Dumped the clothes and went back to the sign and, without giving myself time to think, I went down the stairs and went in.

The office is the basement of one of those old three-family flats and it is one shabby, beat-up place. The walls are crumbling rock, cracked masonry and a sort of stucco which is beginning to disintegrate. Parts of the ceiling are bare under-flooring and parts have some ceiling tile nailed up. Pipes run across the ceiling and down the walls. There are two battered wooden tables, one battered old-fashioned desk and about a dozen chairs, straight wooden kitchen ones and rickety folding ones.

And there were people. People in the chairs, people at the tables, people pinning things to the bulletin board leaning against the wall. Some were beaded and bearded, some were clean-shaven; some were girls with long flowing tresses in long flowing dresses, some were girls with enormous eyeglasses and tiny skirts. They were all young. And as I looked at them I could feel moss sprouting out of my ears and I backed up and would've (I think) scrambled out of there if a young black man sitting at the table nearest the door had not looked up and seen me.

He smiled and got up and came over to me. He said, Hi. It couldn't be you came to work, could it?

That so caught me off-guard that I blurted out that I had.

Thank Christ, he said and he took my arm and led me to the desk where the phone was still ringing. It had been ringing ever since I came in. If you'd just answer this damn phone (he said). This mimeo will tell you a few things. Anything you can't answer, tell them to come in or call back tomorrow. OK?

So I said OK and I answered the phone all afternoon. All I could do was give the address and the hours of the Center, the official name is The Draft Resistance Center, and a few routine facts from the sheet, but at least it kept the phone from going unanswered.

When I left, the young man (Gabriel is his name) gave me some material to study. There is a lot to learn. Not only does one need to know the entire draft procedure, the exemptions and deferments and procedures for filing, but also how to interview the kids so as to find out exactly where they are and what can be done for them.

I liked it there. There was a very good feeling about the place, I guess partly because everybody believes in what he is doing. The purpose, resisting the draft, is certainly one reason it is attractive to me. But also it was the kids. Even though I've got one foot in the grave, I felt at home with them. When I said goodbye to Gabriel (the young black man), I felt as if I were saying goodbye to a friend.

Monday, Sept. 29

A dark, depressing day. I awoke at 6 when the alarm went off (J. was catching an 8 o'clock plane) and when I saw the gray curtain of rain outside I put the pillow over my head and tried to go back to sleep. If I hadn't had to see Ames's adviser I might've stayed there all day.

The day (last Fri.) at the Draft Counseling Center seemed like a crazy dream. What did I think I was doing there . . . a middle-aged old biddy in among those bright young chicks? Maybe they *seemed* not to notice my decrepitude but they would in time and what 18-yr.-old wants to discuss his draft problems with somebody old enough to be his mother? It seemed to me, lying there under the pillow, that I was crazy to think I could crawl out of my cave into this sunlit young world. And I decided I would not go back.

But I did have to go to Ames's school. So I got up and tried to pull myself together. I was standing on my head when I happened to glance at the mirror on the closet door (usually the door is shut so I can't see myself) and as I looked at my up-ended self, I said aloud, You are old, Father William, and your hair has become very white; and yet you incessantly stand on your head. Do you think, at your age, it is right?

I am truly one of the world's most ludicrous specimens. Me and my articles of faith . . . this headstand business, for just one. I started standing on my head maybe twenty years ago (I don't even remember why) and I feel that as long as I continue to stand on my head, all is not yet lost. (I also try to avoid stepping on cracks even though Mother's back is no longer around to be broken.)

As I was leaving, I remembered the stuff the young man at the Center gave me to study and I took it to drop off later and explain that I couldn't come back.

Ames's counselor is a rather attractive young man. Pink-cheeked, with a funny little black beard that doesn't quite cover his chin, curly black hair that covers his head, ears, and most of his forehead. It seemed funny to be calling this infant Mr. Samuels. He clearly could not understand why I had come. He said Ames is at the top of all her classes; that she *is* somewhat shy but is well-liked by everybody.

I told him something must be wrong because she wants to quit school. He had had no idea that she was not perfectly content and he ruminated on this and finally said that perhaps the work is not challenging enough and she is not getting ego-satisfactions. (I cringed at hearing Ass Bird's tainted lingo from this fresh-faced young man). He then said he would try having her tutor some of the kids who are having trouble with Russian. She's very good at languages, he said.

We agreed to keep in touch and now I must try to shelve my worries and see what happens.

Went to the Draft Center hoping to slip in and leave the material saying I was sorry but I was over-committed (I dislike that word but it's useful). I opened the door on Bedlam. The phone was ringing and nobody was answering it, there were lines in front of the tables and all of the waiting chairs were filled. Gabriel, the kindly young black guy, was at one of the tables and when I edged up to try to speak my piece, he grabbed onto me and said, Thank Christ! Take the phone, will you?

Then he went right back to work and I couldn't interrupt him so I answered the phone all afternoon.

At the end of the day when Gabriel had swept out the last of the kids, only he and I were left and I told him about how I was overcommitted.

His lips tightened and his face closed up and he

said, Well, I hadn't pegged you for one of those.

One of what? I asked.

One of those nice ladies who can't take the dirty hippie types with their dirty language and all. We've had plenty of them and they usually last one day. But I didn't see you like that.

I tried to tell him it wasn't that. It's really (I said) that I do have a lot of other things to do and I have a family and . . . well, I just don't have the time.

Sure, sure, he said. Not even one afternoon a week.

That made me kind of mad and before I thought I said, Oh, for Christ's sake! I'm too old for this! Can't you see that?

Is that what's bugging you? he asked. Is it that for real? I said it was.

What do you think? he said. The kids come here to screw the counselors? Who you think cares how old you are?

I care, I said.

Well, he said, if that's what you care about then you better go on home and sit with your hang-up. Then, his face changed and he smiled. Look, Sophie (he said), what we getting into a hassle about? You say you're too old, I say you're not. You got time, try it. Later, if you find kids backing off, saying No thanks, Grandma, then you quit. OK?

What could I say? And as I drove home I was grateful to Gabriel for talking me into staying. What's the use of standing on my head if I'm going to sit home nursing my hang-up??

Monday, Oct. 6

Very busy at the Center. There is so much to do, with answering the ever-ringing phone, interviewing the kids, making calls, looking up things, that the paper work is sorely slighted. Everybody says we should have some idea of the percentages of success or failure of the various kinds of cases. But nobody has time to pull stuff out of the files and work on it.

Also, there are émigrés and deserters with whom the Center corresponds and this too is falling behind. The other day at what might be called a business meeting (a group of us who were emptying ashtrays, rinsing coffee cups, sweeping the floor and sorting papers), I volunteered to take over the correspondence for a while. Spent most of yesterday reading and answering letters from kids in Montreal, Stockholm and London. Some of them are lonely, most of them are homesick (particularly the ones in Stockholm) and all of them are having a rough time. I wrote to two today whose parents have almost literally turned their pictures to the wall and have nothing to do with them.

Gabriel continues to be helpful and friendly. They are *all* helpful and friendly but I have more to do with Gabriel because he is there every day and the others come irregularly. Also, he usually comes in in the afternoon as do I and we close up the place together.

He's a grad. student (working for his Ph.D. Something about Negroes in the Reconstruction) and safe from the draft. Said he had gotten off on account of his head. I asked him what was wrong with it and he said, Well, I had a head problem but not much of one. I mean, I was uptight about the war but no more than anybody else, I guess, and I'm kind of nonviolent though I'm not strictly a pacifist. I saw this shrink at the clinic and after a couple of months he gave me a letter and well, I accepted the deferment. So now (he said smiling) I got this load of guilt, see, so like that's why I'm here.

I like the way he talks. Slightly Southern but just a touch, it is also gentle and with a kind of undertone in it as if he could talk another way but he likes to kid around. It gives everything he says a kind of twist as if he were laughing at himself.

Gave him a lift home the other day, not that he couldn't have walked it, but just for the friendliness of it. And he asked me to come in for a cup of coffee. So I did. He lives in one of those falling-down old tenements near where they are being urbanly renewed. It's broken up into a lot of rooms. His room shares the bath with the 4 others on his floor. He has a hot plate and an old-fashioned fridge, a single couch-bed, two chairs and a table and a lot of books. Oh, yes, and a record player.

I asked him what he lives on and he said his fellowship and also his mother sends him some sometimes. I don't drink or smoke, pot or cigarettes, he said, so all I need is books and I steal some of those.

Why, I used to do that, I said. And I told him about the BLG (for Book Lifting Group) that we had in college. The members were assigned a book (or 2 or whatever) that we were to lift from the bookstore. It was for the benefit of the members who couldn't afford to buy books.

Were you one of the ones who couldn't afford to buy? Gabriel asked.

Well, no, I said. Actually I could afford to. And I was sitting there wondering why I had not been able to say that I was poor, to tell the little unimportant lie that would've put me more in his world, when I heard him laugh.

Don't you feel bad, Sophie, Gabriel said. You like me with the draft. You paid your dues like I'm paying mine.

I stared at him, hardly able to believe my ears. Imagine somebody, and almost a stranger at that, having that kind of understanding. What a very nice guy Gabriel is. Nice-looking too. He is a combination of the best of the red, white and black . . . The Indigenous American. He reminds me of somebody, I can't think who.

At dinner Ames was so agreeable that I became slightly unhinged and babbled like an idiot. I was so grateful, so pathetically grateful that she was treating me as if I were almost human.

How weirdly like a love affair is this relationship with the first-born. At least if the child is a girl and you're her mother. Maybe it's that way with some fathers too but not with J. He never seems to feel the terrible loss I feel about Ames as I see her move further and further away from us, particularly me. I used to get angry and resentful and hurt but I am learning to control it some, although I still get hurt, just about every damn day. I know it's growth for her but it's a kind of death for me. When I said that to J. he called me a monster.

Don't you want her to grow up? he said in letters ten feet tall.

Sure I do, I said sniveling into my Kleenex. Only (I said) she's growing away from US.

That's only natural, said Our Sage.

So's death, said the Wailing Wall.

And the Sage phlumped a big phlump and disappeared into his study.

There I was bleeding from every pore and he tells me it's only natural. Screw the cold-hearted bastard. But that's just what I don't seem able to do. I tried one night not so long ago but it was just gymnastics, no friendliness at all.

I have this terrible ache inside, it sits in me like a stone. I told Ass Bird and he said why didn't I tell J. about it? I said I'd tried but J. hasn't a glimmer. Actually, AB has even less than that. Once I said (to AB), If J. would just call me by my name sometimes! And AB wanted to know why my name is so important to me.

How did AB ever get into this profession?? When I think of kind, intelligent, loving Dr. Damon I wonder how I can continue with this thick-headed idiot. How I loved Dr. Damon and how good he was to let me think he loved me. So good that I still remain convinced after all these years that he did care about me. If only he weren't so far away. Still, maybe I could go out and see him. But maybe he doesn't practice anymore (that was, after all, nearly 20 years ago). Or maybe he is . . . oh, do not think it . . . dead.

Thursday, Oct. 9

Dear Divorce Court: Can This Marriage Be Saved?

I've got a depression you could use to hang coats on. J. and I had interc. the other night and it wasn't very good. In fact it was terrible. It wasn't that there was not for me the Big O which Deb is always saying is so important. I can do without that but there was nothing . . . just NOTHING.

I had gone to bed feeling lonely and tired and wishing somebody would hold my hand like that man in the Fr. movie. So I put out my hand and took J.'s (I knew he was awake) and in 3 seconds he was all over me and there was my hand just lying empty. I cried afterwards (I am becoming a veritable Niagara) and he said stiffly that he was sorry his love-making was not up to my standards. I felt sorry for him but when I came back from the bathroom he was asleep and then I felt even sorrier for myself..

He's in D.C. again. Today, tomorrow and the next day. Ass Bird asked me why I don't go with him sometimes. I told him I had gone a couple of times but it wasn't worth it. Those guys do everything together. They eat together, they take taxis together, they even go to the john together. I told AB I felt like Back Stage Wife, hanging around outside the men's room for a glimpse of my husband, that being the only place I knew he'd have to go sometimes.

AB had never heard of Back Stage Wife, wanted to know who she was.

Listen, I said (and I said it very seriously), you are too young for me.

He asked me how old I thought he was.

I don't care how old you are, I said. You are too young for me.

If only I could talk to somebody who understands something! Somebody who likes me (as I know Ass Bird positively does not), likes ME . . . Sophie . . . not what I can do, not what I say, not just my fine mind nor my not-quite-yet-decayed body . . . but all of those and whatever else goes to make up ME.

David is coming home this weekend. I dread it. His letters are awful. He was always rather staid but he sounds now like a perfect prig. How can he have got this way in just 14 years? It takes most people at least 40 years.

Monday, Oct. 13

Last night was a great mess. A lot of it was my fault but some of it at least was David's. I don't feel as bad about it as I did last night but I still find it hard to believe I am related by blood to that boy. Let alone that I am his mother.

It began with a restrained-type argument about Vietnam between the three of us . . . J., David and me (Ames was at Gretchie Stein's as usual). But when David began talking about the necessity for "guarantees" before we could get out, I saw red, green and purple and I began banging on the table and raising my voice. J. told me to quiet down and I yelled at him and to my amazement burst into tears and ran up to the bathroom. I was in there trying to swallow some Calm-all which is of course a fraud, but I am at the point now where I would welcome the ministrations of a competent quack (as opposed to those of the incompetent bona fide Dr. AB).

Anyway, I was there, gagging on the Calm-all, when J. knocked and asked what I was doing in there. I said I was disemboweling myself. Then he said to please come down as David wanted to apologize. Which I did and D. gave out with a stiff gray-flannel apology which I accepted in the same spirit in which it was tendered . . . i.e., unwillingly.

Later David and I got more friendly and we watched something on TV about the God-awful plight of the American Indian. Then at one point David said in a patronizing voice, That's another thing your generation has to answer for.

MY generation?? I said coldly. I beg your pardon but I was not a contemporary of General Custer.

Then he said (and I want to remember all this right), Well, but you haven't done anything to help the situation, have you? I mean, you and all the rest of your generation got us into all this . . . poor Indians, pollution and lung cancer, racism and riots and Vietnam. I mean, somebody has to be responsible, don't they? Or don't you believe in moral responsibility?

I tell you, I looked at that 14-year-old fiend in human form and I could hardly believe it. Then I shut my eyes hard and tried to remember he is only a child and my own baby. Then I opened my eyes and tried to reason. I said that every generation receives the good and bad consequences of the acts of all the generations before it (which may not be exactly true but is true enough). And, with what I thought was inspiration, I cited that now hackneyed thing of Donne's which David used to love when he was young and lovable. You should say (I said) that no *generation* is an island, entire unto itself (I skipped the middle), I am involved in mankind, therefore never send to know for whom the bell tolls . . .

Then I sat back and watched a look of acute embarrassment spreading over his face as he said, That's a lot of sentimental crap, Mom.

All I was trying to say (I said) is that my generation *is* involved, that we do have a sense of responsibility and that we care very much.

Oh, *caring*, he said. Lots of people *care* but they don't do anything. I'm talking about concrete action, Mom, not something in your heart or mind.

That's where action begins, I told him. And the caring which you so despise leads to very real action. What's needed is not less caring but more.

That's old leftist liberalism, the vicious child said. That's out and a good thing, too. What good did it ever do?

So, admiring my restraint, I told him in a calm voice that it was old leftist liberals who had finally achieved the decision in Brown vs. the Board of Education.

What's that? he wanted to know.

Jesus! I said (feeling like everybody in the world is too young for me). It's the school desegregation decision, that's all. And back before that it was crappy old liberals who got unions recognized and child labor laws and minimum wage standards. And fatheaded black and white leftists who sat in restaurants and got their heads broken.

Yea, Mom, he said. But all that's ancient history. I mean, people like *you* never did anything.

Actually some of us did. (I tried to be mild but I was feeling about as mild as a maddened adder.) Your Grandmother Margaret who never had to wash a dish or make a bed in her life spent some time in jail for working at a birth control clinic that dispensed diaphragms.

Diagrams? the retarded boy said.

Diaphragms, I said. They're a sort of stone age birth control device and it was against the law to dispense them. But she did and she went to jail, not for long but . . .

Granny? In jail? He was astounded. Then he collected himself and said more calmly, But that's all about a hundred years ago.

Your father and I are not a hundred years ago and when he was in graduate school and I was in college we circulated petitions to get McCarthy impeached. Not that McCarthy (I said, seeing his face). There was another McCarthy, *Joe* McCarthy. He was a sort of home-grown Hitler. Communists and Bleeding-Heart Liberals were his Jews and some of us were out with petitions to try to get him out of the Senate.

Petitions, the boy said, curling his lip. Nothing very hard about going around with petitions.

You don't always have to have been jailed or beaten up. Although once I did get into a sort of fight. It was when I was picketing Woolworth's.

What were you picketing *Woolworth's* for?

Integration. It was almost always integration back then. And I was picketing with a black girl named Nona when a man, a white man, came up to her and started saying dirty things . . . obscene and racist at the same time. I hit him over the head with my sign which couldn't have hurt him much but he shoved me up against the store window and Nona kicked him and the cop who had been just standing there arrested Nona and me.

You went to JAIL? He sounded appalled, almost stunned.

I said I wished I could say I did but I didn't. I called J. from the station house and he came and we weren't even booked.

OK, Mom, I admit that was pretty revolutionary for those days but what good did it do? I mean, if it had done any good we wouldn't be where we are today. It must've done *you* some good, but not society as a whole. Well, nothing has changed, has it?

But I'm just *telling* you (I could feel a piece of my head blow off and hit the ceiling) that things *have* changed, that good *was* done . . .

Well . . . (he was, I think, still trying to be patient but I didn't give him any credit for that or anything else by then) but that's not the way to get things done. Not anymore, anyway. We've got to have power blocs now. For example, to manipulate the black power groups so they'll cooperate with other groups.

Manipulate? Who's going to do the manipulating?

The sane white power structure, he said. Plus, of course, any sane blacks who want to be included in.

I see. The white establishment will let in the Uncle Toms and you'll manipulate the others by shooting up some of them and putting the rest in concentration camps. There was a name once for people like you and it's FASCIST.

J. came busting in from his study and looked at us both and said, What in hell's going on here?

It's Mom, the traitorous boy said. She can't argue without blowing her top.

This boy, I said to J., this boy here thinks you and I and the rest of us are washed up, finished . . . with our leftist liberalism and our petitions and strikes and sit-ins. It was all for nothing, never did a bit of good. The world we made, the world we've given them is going to hell in a hack and they're going to save it by working with the good niggers and manipulating the wild jigaboos. I tell you, this child ought to be taken out of that fascist school and put in a House of Correction.

Oh, hell, Mom (both David and I were standing by now and glaring at each other). You're as nutty as all those little old ladies in white tennis shoes.

Now, wait a minute, J. said to him.

Oh, shut up. (I said it to J. but I was looking at David in all his once sweet half-manly pinkness). And then I said directly to David, *And to think I stopped smoking for you.* (And I felt all the top of my head blow right off.)

Calm down, the Peacemaker said. But I whipped around him and went to the closet for my coat.

Where do you think you're going? J. asked.

I know he meant well but I hate to be asked where I *think* I'm going.

I'm going out to shoot up the white power structure, I said. And I went.

I drove around awhile and tried to think. But I

had nothing to think with. I had lost my head back there in the living room. I began to be ashamed of myself and my unseemly (as David would think and he'd be right) performance. But that didn't change the fact that David seemed headed for damnation. And I kept thinking where did we go wrong? Or was it maybe That School which I had opposed on the general grounds that prep schools were likely to lead ultimately to Wall St. But David had wanted to go (a bad sign right there) and J. had pointed out that *he* had gone to prep school and had not ended on Wall St.; arguing the while that there is nothing inherently wrong with Wall St.

So I drove around and around and wished I had somebody to talk to. Started towards Deb's but thought of all her troubles and how she does not need mine and also, truth to tell, how I didn't need anymore of hers right then. Anyhow, I knew she'd likely be 7 sheets to the wind and I can't take her when she's falling into the furniture and going on about the days when she and Marsden were married.

Then I thought of Gabriel. Despite the generation abyss, we seem to have become friends and I knew he wouldn't care what time it was if he were home and I knew he wouldn't be getting drunk. And, maybe most importantly, I knew he wouldn't think I am a little old lady in white tennis shoes.

I drove around a while more, trying to get up my courage to call him because of course he could be busy with his friends (or a friend) or I could have misjudged his friendliness and he could just think I am a Graybeard Loon and not want to be bothered with me.

Finally I decided to leave it to Fate. If a telephone booth should appear before I got to Mass. Ave. I would call him. (It was a perfectly fair test because I was in the wilds of Somerville and had no idea where any phone booths were.)

In a very short time Fate not only produced a telephone but one that was working. Gabriel was home and no, he was not busy and yes, he'd meet for a cup of coffee but why didn't I come there and he'd give me coffee?

So I did.

We had coffee and I told him about David, not anywhere near all of it but some of the worst. He said it is not my fault; David is a kid and this a stage and he will get over it and I take it too seriously and I should not get uptight about it and other reassuring things.

And then I told him about that last exchange and David's saying I am like a little old lady in white t. shoes and he started to laugh. But then I told him about my saying to think I stopped smoking for him and Gabriel howled. Walked around the room holding his sides and finally ended up rolling on the floor, with tears coming out of his eyes.

It's plain to see you never smoked, I said to him. Then, as he kept on rolling around and laughing, I said loudly, Listen, I did do it for him. I was pregnant with that wicked boy when the stuff about smoking came out and I stopped so as not to injure that delicate little creature inside me.

And still he laughed.

Listen! (I got on my knees and started shaking him.) You don't know what it was like! I mean to tell you, every day I got up and climbed up on the cross. I gained hundreds of pounds, not counting the ones I'd gained just by being pregnant. I've even got stigmata, great white lines on my stomach and hips from gaining all that weight.

He didn't believe it. You could never have been fat, he said.

I said that's how much he knew. I looked like a bloated old bull frog, I said. Imagine a runt like me weighing 130 lbs.

He said he couldn't. But (he said) you're not a runt. You're just the right size.

That made me feel good. Of course, after all these years I've gotten used to being small and I don't think about it anymore. But, still, as everybody grows so much (both David and Ames are way taller than I am) I seem to be shrinking. Five feet two and a half is not, after all, a midget but it's not much in a world where girls 16 years old wear size nine shoes and have the height to match (Ames is five seven). And J. who is over 6 ft. used to look at me when we were walking (in the days when we still walked) as if I were deliberately being short in order to provoke him and he'd say, Can't you walk a *little* faster?

We got up off the floor and we decided we were hungry so we walked to the Chinese place and had egg rolls and sweet and sour. Thank God he has the grace not to try to pay for me. We just split the check. As we were walking back to his place (where my car was) he said, You oughta think about black power and whether you'd trust a bunch of dumb niggers to tell you what to do any more'n you'd trust a bunch of dumb whites.

Why *dumb* niggers? I asked.

What do you call Geo. Wallace and Thurmond and those who're selling white power? Intelligent?

No, I said, but what the blacks are doing is different.

You want to tell me how, Sophie-girl?

We were at the car now and as I got in I said I'd think about it and try to come up with an answer. Then I thanked him for the coffee and for letting me spill my troubles out on him.

Anytime, he said. Then he reached in the window and patted me on the head and said, Stay cool, baby.

It was 12:30 when I got home and David had left to take the bus back to That School. There was a note on the table saying Deb had called and to call her back. I crept upstairs but J. was awake, propped up with all the pillows reading a stack of papers (he never reads real books).

You all right? he asked and I said I was. He asked where I'd gone and I said to see a friend from the Center.

Then he said I must never (and he underlined NEVER) get into anything like that with David again. He was very upset (J. said). He was afraid you might go out and kill yourself.

Oh, the poor kid, I said, sitting down suddenly at the foot of the bed. I must have been terrible. I know I was pretty bad, but I didn't know I was that bad.

You have to remember David is practically an infant (J. said) and he doesn't know how to take the high-powered emotionalism you dish out. Speaking of which, your friend Deb is in a state. I don't advise you to call her tonight.

I said I had to, especially if she's in a state.

Then you'll never come to bed, he said looking sour.

And he was very nearly right. I almost never did get to bed. Deb was weeping and raging. Marsden had come over to discuss the business of Kathy's school. He had agreed to pay tuition for one more year and then they'd discuss it again. So things were fairly friendly until he made what Deb called some dirty cracks about her housekeeping. Apparently he practically called her a slob.

I sympathized of course but inwardly I was rather pleased, hoping that this kind of treatment might cut the tie that binds her to him.

But no. Before the conversation ended Deb was crying about the good old days when she and Marsden made love on a mud-tracked kitchen floor surrounded by dirty dishes, children's boots and a hamper of diapers. She said that Molly has ruined him but she, Deb, thinks he could still be reclaimed. By guess who?

Somewhere around three, her voice gave out and I crawled up to bed so tired I could not brush my teeth.

Thursday, Oct. 16

Yesterday was Moratorium Day. There were marches and speeches all over and an especially large rally here. The kids at the Center marched with whatever groups they hang out with. Gabriel organized a group from a ghetto high school where he used to do volunteer teaching and he marched with them. J. canceled classes but he did not march . . . not productive enough, I suppose. Ames's school went together. Hallie P. asked me to come over and march with a group in Newton but I said I had arranged to go with another group. A barefaced lie since I have been very careful not to arrange anything with anybody. For reasons which I don't understand I wanted to march by myself . . . a silent piece of the whole.

I started out at the Square and listened to the speeches there which I found singularly unmoving and I trudged into town to the Common, seeing along the way, either in the line of march or on the side, dozens of people I know. Somehow managed to avoid getting hooked up with any one of them.

There were some good speakers at the Common but long before it was over I began to get that old claustrophobic feeling (AB says this is simple anxiety which is academically interesting but not very helpful) as I thought of being jammed in the subway with all those thousands of people after the rally. The impossibility of getting a cab and the ghastly alternative of walking all the way back to Cambridge made me hotfoot it to the then-uncrowded subway and so home.

I was watching the rally on blessed Channel 2 when the phone rang and it was Cissy. She said, Oh, so your rally *is* over. I thought it would be.

I said it wasn't but that I had got tired and had come on home. I asked her if it wasn't about time for the march to start out there.

She said yes, but she wasn't going; she was sick of marches. I am sick of everything, Sophie, she said. Suppose I just ran away, would you take me in?

I said she needn't ask but what in hell was wrong.

She said she is still worried about Soph but it is Alex that is her immediate problem.

Alex and his kookie kids (she said) and his beads and his bells and his diets! My God, Sophie, he has some of these Godhead kids stashed in the basement! And the store is going to pieces. I went in there yesterday and fired the lot of them. I closed up for today of course, but tomorrow I'm going to have to go in and run the place.

I asked what she thought had taken possession of Alex. He always seemed so gentle and sweet and sane, I said.

He's never been sane, she said. What's happened is his own weird reaction to the male menopause, at least I suppose it's that unless he really is crazy. He's losing his hair and he thinks he's losing his virility and this is his way of proving he's as good as he ever was. Why are men so dumb? You married the only sane man in this world. I hope you know that?

I said I guessed J. was pretty sane. But that maybe he stays sane because he's so blind he doesn't see what's going on around him.

What're you talking about? Cissy demanded. Why, I've known that man almost as long as you have and he is not blind.

Just knowing him (I said) is not the same as being married to him.

What *is* the matter with you? Cissy said. J. is a paragon.

Usually Cissy can say anything to me (and often she does) and I don't get mad but this got to me and I said, You'd think J. was some saint and I a lowly sinner hardly fit to touch the hem of his robe when, to tell you the truth, Cissy, that man is just about driving me to put my head in the oven.

Then there must be something wrong with your head, she said not at all sympathetically. Is he screwing bell ringers in the cellar? Is he growing a hideous orange beard? Is he chanting Hare Krishna all day?

I said, That's not the only way to ruin a marriage. You can just never be home, you can be deaf, dumb and blind.

Oh, Sophie! Cissy said, interrupting me impatiently. Why don't you grow up? Nobody's got the kind of ESP you expect. Why don't you try to fit in with his life instead of expecting him to fit yours?

Then suddenly she was very serious, and she said, Does he still want to sleep with you?

And I said, Yes, more's the pity.

You mean *you* don't want to, she said. Well, Sophie, you'd better shape up or you're not going to keep that good husband.

I said I didn't much care if I didn't.

Then you're a fool, she said.

I felt like crying but I hate people who cry over the phone . . . makes the other guy feel so helpless . . . so I did not but said, Maybe I am but I am also a human being and I cannot live with somebody who treats me as if I were paper on the wall.

She sighed. Then she said that I expected too much of everybody and of myself too. She said my standards were impossibly high and I overreacted to everything and I should take it easy and "slop along with the rest of humanity." Then she broke off and laughed and said, You *are* a good girl, you know that? Here I have been pointing out all your warts to you and you sit there and take it.

I said she had given me good advice and I was sorry I hadn't helped *her* any, that I had not meant to wrench the conversation around to me.

She said she had done the wrenching and the talk had done her a world of good and for me to take it easy.

I told her to do the same and then I came away from the phone to brood on all she said.

And I decided she is right. I am a long-faced, dreary slob and I never make any overtures. I only sit sullenly waiting for J. to think of asking *me* to do something. So (I decided) I must make the first moves and I must start by forgetting old grudges and being friendly and cheerful.

So when he came home, I had ice in the bucket and I offered to fix his drink and I asked him how things were.

He looked a little surprised as he said thanks very much. And as I mixed the drink he said things were bad but he supposed they could get worse.

I asked him what new was bad and he said he was caught in the middle, trying to talk to the students and being too moderate for them and trying to talk to the faculty and being too radical for *them*.

I asked about a faculty resolution that he'd been backing . . . in re getting out of Vietnam . . . and what had happened to it.

He brightened up (which should have warned me but it didn't) and said it was being circulated now and he showed me a copy of it.

I read it and said the idea was great but the style certainly left a lot to be desired.

He wanted to know what was wrong with the style. And I (still blind) said it was crawling with clichés.

He said, Thank you very much. And he yanked the paper out of my hands.

It turns out of course that he wrote it.

Well, how was I to know? And it certainly *was* chock-full of phrases like "these troubled times" and "taking a stand" and "not letting grass grow under our feet." But then I thought of what Cissy would say: that the style was none of my business and what did it matter? And I decided she would be right so I said I was sorry and that the IDEA was simply great and I hoped it would get the votes it should.

Ames came in and made herself a sandwich and dashed out so J. and I were alone at dinner.

After listening to all the bad news on the TV I asked J. if he would like to go to a movie. He looked surprised (I guess I *don't* often make suggestions) and said he would, only there is a committee meeting tonight.

After he went off Deb called and asked if I'd go to a symposium on the population problem and I said sure. It was a far cry from the cozy evening I'd had in mind but I figured it would at least get me out of the house and maybe keep me from building up a federal case against J.

It was a public thing at the medical school and very well attended. There were two famous authorities whose names everybody knows (and which I now cannot remember) and two other gents, a biologist and an anthropologist. The biologist was an elderly man with stooped shoulders, a lined craggy face, thinning white hair and he is my Dream Man from now on. He was intelligent and informative and concerned but they all were that. This great man was also funny, witty and so alive that you felt he reached out and touched you. The subject is, God knows, depressing; the art of contraception being very backward and nowhere practiced as much as it should be and my hero didn't attempt to mitigate this. But where the others made me feel hopelessly depressed, the great man left me feeling aware of the reason for the depression but rising above it with a kind of cosmic hope.

They spoke of course of the Pill, on which I have been relying all these years, and apparently it is not only a very crude method . . . like killing a mosquito with a sledgehammer, one man said . . . but has potential dangers as well. But, as the great man pointed out, so does childbirth.

I came away with a mixture of feelings: heartened by the words and the spirit of my hero, depressed by the seemingly unstemmable rising tide of people and personally sad that, in a few years, the problem of contraception will not exist for me. That, indeed, it is much too late for me to entertain any fancies of having more children. One of the gents said that the percentage of Mongoloid children born to women over 40 is significantly high. But also I know I haven't the patience, energy and will to get through those first 5 or 6 years of infancy and childhood. As Dr. Whatchamacallit said, Love alone is not enough.

Deb seemed in good shape; says there are some things she rather enjoys about being alone. We stopped for a sandwich and coffee and she was very funny about the joys of spinsterhood, little things like having the whole bed and not finding shaving foam all over the mirror and socks and underwear all over the floor. I laughed and agreed there were many compensations but I said I did not think I was cut out to live alone.

She looked surprised and said she thought I was the most independent person she knew. There's J. (she said) forever off to some meeting or other and you seem perfectly cheerful and contented. I always thought you and J. had a very special relationship.

I told her we did and that it was not generally known but I would let her in on it; that J. was studying to be a monk in that Thomas Merton order where they don't talk. He'll be accepted any day now (I said) and when he goes in, I'll join the Little Sisters of the Poor.

She laughed but it is not really so much of a joke.

When I came in J. was working at his desk and I asked him how the meeting had gone. He told me some about it; especially that Ben W. who is one of our oldest friends had walked right by him without speaking.

I could hardly believe this and I asked what had happened.

Feelings are very high, he said. And Ben thinks we should only act as individuals and the universities should not take any political position.

I said everybody and every institution took a position on this war whether it was an official position or not. Then I said I was shocked at Ben.

Oh, no, said J. He's doing what he thinks is right and there is a lot to be said for his position. But we start from different premises and I'm afraid that he's going to end where I am now.

Why "afraid"? I asked.

Because, he said, it will mean things have gotten a lot worse.

I said I didn't see how they could help but get worse when the country is run by bastards with no principles and no intelligence.

He said I must not make the mistake of thinking Nixon is stupid.

I said I didn't see how it could be intelligent to

divide the country into armed camps; that he couldn't govern nor be reelected in a country torn apart.

He can, J. said, if he is willing to be repressive enough.

You mean more suspension of civil rights? More harassment of liberals and radicals, more phony trials and jailings?

J. said he would not be surprised.

And suddenly I saw the campuses covered with ROTC's and the National Guard patrolling the streets and paddy wagons pulling up in the dead of night and hauling people off and maybe the White House being burned . . . just a little . . . by the CIA, and martial law being declared and all the Black Panthers, and Spock and Coffin and Saint Ramsey Clark being taken in for questioning or for protective custody . . . and nothing to be done.

And I said, Then we're lost and there's nothing to be done. Nothing at all.

Don't be silly, he said, pushing his chair back and stretching. There are lots of ways to fight and lots of people fighting.

Then he got up and sighed and said, Oh my God, I am so *tired.*

And we went to bed and I didn't really mind the interc. It seemed the least I could do for a man on the ramparts. And I held him tightly, tightly not so much out of affection as to keep him from that concentration camp I could see ahead.

This morning when the alarm went off, I got up dazedly (still with my reclamation project in mind) with the idea of making breakfast but J. pushed me back and said it was way too early; that he was catching a plane.

I asked if he'd be back for dinner. He said he hoped so and he would call before six if he could not make it.

He did not call by six so I turned down Frances L.'s invitation to the opening of some new play and I prepared a fine dinner. Which I heated and reheated and finally, about nine, shoved in the fridge. He came in at eleven all cheerful because it looks as if the Rockefellers might give him some money for one of his ghetto projects. I asked why he didn't call which was mean because I knew damn well what the answer would be and it was: he had thought he said that if he was *coming back* he would call before six.

One would not think that I could be so small as to hold this against him. But one would be wrong. He has gone to bed and I am sitting here in the guest room writing this with the strong feeling that no matter what I do I cannot make things any better between us.

It seems to me we are hopelessly at odds. I have thought on all Cissy said but even if I agree that I am childish and demanding and "overreactive" (as AB says), I cannot change myself completely to fit J.'s life and personality. I would still feel short-changed every time I turn around and the only way I can stop feeling that is to stop caring what happens to us. And if I could do *that,* then I could not give even the minimum sexual compliance (which is all I seem to be good for) required to keep J. going. So where are we?

Cissy is right as far as she goes but she does not go far enough. And to say somebody's feelings are silly is no answer. Silly feelings are as real as any others and for those who have them just as important. Besides which, I don't really think my feelings are silly.

But, whether they are or not, the diagnosis would seem to be that I am a misfit and I suppose the prescription would be: help. But I have been crying *au secours* for a long time and I am beginning to have the strong conviction that there is NOBODY OUT THERE.

Monday, Oct. 20

Today at the Center things were quiet so when Gabriel came in and said, What do you think? Mae West *and* W. C. Fields are playing. We went. It was "My Little Chickadee." First time he'd seen it. It was maybe my second (or third) but it seemed new.

One funny thing: the kids (and they were mostly all kids) sat with their arms around each other, and partway through Gabriel's arm went around my shoulders in a loose and casual drape. I froze for a minute, thinking how shocking this was: a 25-year-old boy and a middle-aged old married woman sitting like this. But then as the arm just stayed there and he continued to look at the movie and laugh, it seemed to me it must be an act of simple friendliness and probably kids do it all the time. If I moved away I would be showing my mind to be an ancient sewer. I mean, *Honi Soit Qui Mal y Pense*. So I relaxed and enjoyed it. It was so nice, as if I were back in school and I was young and hopeful and not outside anymore but with it.

It was a crippling blow to come out at 4:30 and

realize I am neither young nor hopeful and that it was time to go home and turn into a pumpkin again.

Thursday, Oct. 23

Yesterday after a quick lunch in the Square, Gabriel and I were walking back through the Yard when we came upon a ball, a small red rubber ball lying on the path. Gabriel kicked it ahead of us and when I came to it, I kicked it and we kept on like that through the Yard. When we got out on the sidewalk, it rolled into the street and disappeared in the traffic.

Gabriel stood with his hands on his hips, looking after it and he said, Doggone, there goes our good ball.

The kicking of the ball, the look on Gabriel's face, what he said and the way he said it suddenly struck me and I knew what I must've known before: Gabriel reminds me of Bertie Williams. And I said, You are like Bertie Williams.

Gabriel grinned and wanted to know if Bertie was some great soccer player.

I said Bertie was better than that. Bertie (I said) was the brightest, the cleverest, the most fun of anybody in our class and he was my best friend from the time we were in nursery school until the end of the fourth grade. That ball we were just kicking made me think of the stone Bertie and I had. It was just an ordinary little stone that we found on the playground but it must have had some kind of magic for us because we kept it under a bush outside the door and every day when we came out for recess we'd kick the stone across the path to the playground. Then when it was time to go in, we'd kick it back and hide it under the bush. Oh, that boy was my hero. I used to wish he were my brother.

Gabriel laughed and said he was honored and then he spoke of something else.

Afterwards, at the Counseling Center, I kept having this feeling that I had forgotten to do something. While I was on the phone, as I was talking to the kids, this feeling would come over me of something very important that I had not done. And, finally, driving home it hit me. I had wanted to tell Gabriel that Bertie was black.

It is odd this feeling I had (still have) that I was not leveling with Gabriel by not telling him Bertie was black. I would have told him had the conversation gone on but once it was over, I couldn't go back and bring it up again. But why should it matter? The color of Bertie's skin had no significance for me. I don't think I even knew we were different colors until later when he'd gone. But, still, it seems somehow important. Not important to me, but important to Gabriel.

Anyway, that started me thinking of Bertie and all that long time ago. Later, when I went to the Library, I looked him up in the NYTimes Index. He wasn't there. I used to do that in college out in California and he was not in it then. And, in Philadelphia, in high school, I used to look up his father in the telephone book. His father's name was Bertrand also. Bertrand B. Williams. But there was never any Bertrand B. Williams nor any B. B. Williams. I don't think I would ever have called or gotten in touch with him if I had found him. I just wanted to know where he was or *that* he was.

It's funny with all I can remember about him that I can never remember what he actually looked like. I know the color of his skin because I can see his hand . . . it was dark brown . . . grasping the edge of a board or the limb of a tree. And I can see his jacket (or one of them). It was dark green wool and it had a zipper up the front and the hood was lined with brown furry stuff. His sneakers were wonderful. They were high and white and they had little circles of black rubber over the ankles. His hair was short and black and tightly curled. But what was his face like? I do not know. It used to bother me that I could not remember his face.

I've wondered sometimes about that funny school we went to. I know it doesn't exist anymore because I looked for it when I was in Philadelphia for Aunt Martha's 70th. That whole area of old houses, old trees and wide streets has been eaten up by a hideous shopping center. But when did the school stop and what happened to Mrs. Whitted and Mrs. Ralph, the ladies who ran it? I asked Aunt Martha and some of the cousins when I was there but the cousins had never heard of it. Aunt Martha did remember it but she snorted and said, You mean that madhouse your mother persisted in believing was a school and a Quaker school at that?

I said that I remembered it as a very good school and that I knew I had been happy there so it couldn't have been a bad one.

Aunt Martha said I sounded just like my mother used to. Then she said, You may take my word for it, Sophie, it was a very *odd* school.

I suppose it was an odd school for that time. It was very free and easy and we were allowed to express ourselves. Children came and went but there was a small core that stayed all the way through the fourth grade which is where the school ended (and, of course, the reason Bertie and I separated. I went to a girls' school and I don't know where he went).

The most important person in that small core was, to me, Bertie. But I still remember Louise Chin who had a beautiful red kite she would fly on the playground. And Dolores whom I always envied because she had pierced ears and wore little gold earrings. I don't remember the rest of them very well. The others were, I suppose, all white, middle-class proper Philadelphians. All probably WASP's.

I wonder why I am so seldom drawn to WASP's. Unless they are oddballs and so don't seem like WASP's. Sometimes I wonder what happened to my head that I went for such a Solid Citizen as J. But of course it didn't have all that much to do with my head. And he wasn't so solid then. He laughed a lot and sometimes he even talked. I'm sure I loved him then, that we loved each other. Maybe we still do.

I should try harder. Tonight I will try. I will be cheerful and responsive when he comes home and I will have interc. and I will not lie there like an old piece of driftwood. I will positively try tonight.

Friday, Oct. 24

I read what I wrote yesterday morning . . . I will positively try tonight . . . and it is to lie down by the river and weep.

The day was the usual. Grocery shopping, quick throwing together of the house, then to the Center. And there was nothing unusual about J.'s calling at 5:30 to say he was staying to have dinner with some students who wanted to talk to him. I was even glad of that, glad some students are still talking and glad they are talking to J. He's very good with students; friendly, not condescending, much more flexible than he is with, for example, me.

Ames and I ate in the kitchen. We always do when we're alone. She hates dining rooms; says they are middle-class syndromes and should be abolished. She was reserved but relatively friendly. Told me about the bake sale the school is having to raise money for scholarships; wondered what "we" could do. How that "we" did warm me. I said what about croissants? She said great. We decided to make the dough the night before (it has to chill before rolling), then I will do the rolling and baking the morning of the sale (she has to be at school) and bring them over.

I was feeling very cheerful after this and I continued feeling so as I packed and wrapped some books and magazines for the Stockholm resisters. I sent what they requested, all extremely grim stuff, but I also included some Xword puzzles, some New Yorkers, and some Mad magazines to leaven the loaf.

So, when J. came in, not very late, I was still cheerful and I greeted him warmly and asked about the dinner with the students.

He was grumpy. Said people were becoming totally irrational and the meeting had not been productive. (I don't know what that man would do without that word;

things are always productive, or non-productive, or counter-productive.)

I fixed him a drink and he told me that the kids (a few of them black, but most not) had some grievances about the treatment of the waiters (all of whom are students and some of whom are black) in the campus dining rooms.

They claim, he said, that the wage scale is unfair but their chief complaint is that there is discrimination against the black waiters. The charge (he said) rests on the fact that a black waiter was asked by the dining room manager to pick up the manager's shoes at the cobbler's.

Well, I said (in moderate, rational tones), it's true that's only one incident. But if I were a waitress I would not like to be asked to go fetch the boss's shoes.

No, J. said, and you wouldn't do it either and that would be the end of it.

Oh, no, I said (still the voice of Sweet Reason). I might well think I might lose my job if I didn't do it. Or that there'd be reprisals.

That word! J. exploded. That's exactly the word the students used.

I asked what was wrong with the word.

It's so loaded, he said. It's a word used between warring factions. Why must the students, and you, too, assume that everybody is the enemy? Why do you leap to the conclusion that the manager is a racist?

I said it didn't seem to me to require a leap, only a small step; and that I thought it fair to assume the manager was at least very biased.

Then you're as much of a crackpot as the students, he snapped.

I said he must've been a great comfort to them if he called them crackpots.

He said of course he had not called them that. (Then why me?) Grumpy again, he said even the facts were not clear, neither about the wages nor about this incident. The waiter was not there, nor the manager. He said he had told them he would talk to both of them and do some investigating about the wages.

I said (rather nastily) that was very Christian of him.

He said what else did I think he would do?

I said maybe ask one of them to pick up his shoes.

He banged his glass down on the table and said, By God, you're more unreasonable than the students! When it comes to race, you go haywire. What *makes* you so violent on that subject?

I said probably because blacks are second-class citizens and so are women and so I identify with them.

A look of what I think was acute nausea spread over his face and he said that identification was a trite truism.

I said so's the fact that the world is round but some people don't seem to be aware of it yet.

Which was not a very bright observation but it didn't matter because he had gone out to refill his glass and he didn't hear it. When he came back, he said, Well, I have to prepare a seminar. And he took himself off to his study, leaving me with the feeling that a bell had rung and he had dismissed his unproductive class of one.

I came up here and as I got ready for bed I simmered and then I brooded. Then I decided I would not give up and I went down and bearded the bear.

Hey, I said, don't you think it's time to stop?

Without even looking up he said he couldn't; that he hadn't finished.

I hesitated, then I said, Well, when *will* you stop?

He looked up and said angrily, I don't know. Quit nagging at me.

And that was that.

Maybe I didn't try hard enough? Maybe I should have gone down nude and got up on his desk and done a belly dance on his papers? What should I have done? I don't know anything except that right now MAN seems like a four-letter word and I say to hell with them all.

Sunday, Oct. 26

Still feeling let down after last night. We had to do something for J.'s visiting dignitaries so gave a dinner. Had Lorna Myers and Deb for the two D.'s. Hoped Deb wouldn't get tanked and she didn't, just a little sloppy around the edges. Had a Harvard Boy to help. With help like that you are really guaranteed gracious living. He burned all the hot hors d'oeuvres except the little franks which he served with the strings still on them. Still, he tried and he meant well. Which is more than I can say for myself.

I did try to be gay and charming but underneath I did not mean well. I was wishing I could press a button that would cause strobe lights to flash and loud rock music to play. Anything to liven things up. Everybody seemed so dull and cardboardy.

Being, as it was, an economists' evening, there was a lot of talk about the inflation-recession. The Money Guys were discussed and there was considerable jumping up and down on the Friedmanites and what they call the Chicago Hoods.

Economists are a funny bunch. Economics has, after all, no reality, no existence, apart from people. But economists often seem to forget the people and talk as if Economics had some separate existence out there in space. They all do this some of the time but these Moneymen must do it all the time. I see the Chicago Hoods as funny little men with tiny pointed heads looking like people just off a flying saucer.

I did learn one thing. Two men were talking about the stock market and they made some joke about odd lots. And I learned that odd lots are, in the stock market as elsewhere, the very thing you don't want to be. They are the people who own a few shares of this, a few of that. They sell at the bottom and buy at the top. They are clearly not with it, those odd lots, and I had a fellow feeling for them.

Afterwards, J. was feeling expansive; said it had been a good dinner and a fine evening and as he patted me on the behind, I knew what was coming. I tried to jack myself up in the shower by reminding myself of how hard I am to live with, how noble and patient he is and how important interc. is to a man and more along the same lines. I was able to act ½ way human but it was not anything to write home about. Still, I know it is better to cooperate so I am not so guilt-ridden. After all, it's just a warm body he wants. Why should I act like the Guardian of the Holy Grail?

I keep worrying about Ames. Not just because she

is so distant with me but because I think she is lonely and unhappy. She comes in and out as if she were avoiding a process server. Creeps in the back door and dashes right up to her room. She says she's on a diet so she can't eat with us . . . just slops up something quickly in the kitchen. When she isn't at the Steins' which is most of the time. Which really wounds me. I'm pretty sure she's OK physically. And I'm sure she's not on drugs. Not only are there no signs at all but she has said she hates drugs and cigarettes and drinking. The fact that I don't smoke or drink (except the token glass at parties) doesn't help me with her at all. And doesn't help me to help HER. I'm middle-class and middle-aged and, worst of all, her mother. Will she ever let me get a foot in the door again?

Monday, Oct. 27

Last week, AB told me a terrible thing. I asked him to get Dr. Damon's address for me (out of one of those directories he has) and of course he wanted to know why I wanted it.

Because I love him, I said. And I'm going out there and be his handmaiden.

I'm afraid you're too late (AB said, clearly taking pleasure in it). Dr. Damon died two years ago.

I felt as if he'd pulled the chair out from under me and had stomped on me with his ugly thick-soled shoes.

AB then told me that he had studied under Dr. D.

I don't believe it, I said.

He wanted to know why not. And I told him.

Because, I said, you're a cold, unfeeling man and he would never have let you become a psychiatrist. And then I burst into tears.

AB showed his sympathy by shoving the Kleenex box one-half inch nearer me. His stolid expressionless face never changes. I suppose this opaqueness is meant to be objectivity but I keep feeling that nothing happens to his face because nothing happens inside him . . . not only does he not feel but he does not think either.

I have come to dislike his face. It is heavy, and jowly, with eyes which stare from behind his thick glasses the way a fish stares through its tank, mindless and fishy-eyed. There is, actually, nothing wrong with his face that a good human expression would not cure but I have never seen a good human expression on it.

I would leave him except I am so superstitious I am afraid I might really lose my mind if I did. Not that he could tell the difference. He has told me several times that I am pathologically honest. Which shows how little he knows. I am *always* lying. My coming to him and acting like a patient is a lie. I don't like him or trust him and I never believe a word he says unless it is something I have told him first. My whole life is a lie. Where I ought to be, in truth, is shacked up with somebody who would come home to print an underground newspaper and who would call me Sophie and hold my hand all night.

Wednesday, Oct. 29

Deb all morning. There were no classes and she came over for coffee, then that drifted into sherry and finally, finally we went out to lunch.

Sometimes as I listen to Deb I feel as if I had been condemned to listen to an eternal, never-ending soap opera. And people think those daytime serials are not realistic.

It was a relief to get away to the Center where relatively sane people attempt to deal in a relatively sane way with real problems (and ones not of their making).

I do so like the kids there. It is funny how I feel a maternal fondness and yet at the same time feel as if I were one of them. Nobody has yet looked at me as if I were Old Mother Hubbard, maybe because of those glasses I bought the second day. It seemed to me that my eyes were the most aged and ugly things about me so I went to one of the kooky stores and got these plain glasses (just with window glass in them) with large black frames and I wear them most times at the Center. I am always forgetting them when I am with Gabriel and I must remember to keep them on. Incidentally, he was not there today and I missed him.

Tuesday, Nov. 4

Met Gabriel at the Center and afterwards we went to the beer joint. Whenever we go there I always have one beer to keep up with him but today I decided I was going to keep up without the beer and I ordered coffee. Then Gabriel did too. I tried to insist he have his beer but he said he doesn't like it. I asked why he had had it before and he said to keep up with me. Oh life, oh time, oh people.

I told him that as long as we were baring our souls I would really rather have a milk shake. So we canceled the order and went to Brigham's and had milk shakes.

Went home with him to borrow a book and while we were there he gathered up some clothes and asked me if I would keep him company in the Laundromat.

So we sat in the Laundromat and talked. He's been telling me about his friend Vern's place up in the country. Vern bought about ten acres and they are putting up cabins. They've got one up and another almost done so they can go up all winter. Vern lives there now and plans to have a commune going by next summer. Sam (a big, heavy-set guy who looks like a black Rod Steiger and seems to be Gabriel's best friend) goes up every weekend and Gabriel goes pretty often. He has been asking me would I like to go sometime and I've given excuses about being busy and the children, etc; But today I came out and told him.

Gabriel, I said, I am too old. That is the thing.

What kind of people do you hang out with, Sophie, that make you think you're old?

Old people, I said. People my age. I'm 38 (I said, taking a year off my age without blinking an eye . . . so much for Ass Bird's pathological honesty).

You don't look 38, you don't act 38 and you'll never be 38 a day in your life, he said.

I said that was nice to hear but that was my age and I wouldn't fit with his friends.

You fit with me, he said.

I said that was different.

It's different, he said in that funny, quirky way he has. But you'd fit just the same.

I said, Well maybe, and we'd see. And then we dropped it.

Now I wonder what I meant by saying it's different (with him) and I wonder even more what he meant by agreeing that it is. I think *I* meant that he and I started together somewhat as equals at the Center and, if anything, with him in the "older" capacity because he was experienced and I was not. And now, having started that way, he sees the inside of me and not the outside. His friends would start out by seeing the hideous reality. I would be the weird old lady that Gabriel is very kindly helping to cross the street.

Friday, Nov. 7

The Big Question . . . Can This Marriage Be Saved? . . . keeps coming back and back to me.

J. is always out of town and when he is not, he is

busy with meetings, seminars, groups, as well, of course, as with his teaching and the book he has been writing these last ten years. I do have sympathy, even admiration, for the kinds of things he does. The plans to wipe out poverty, the ghettos and ghetto schools; the attempts to bring blacks into the economic life; and, on the international level, to reduce tensions by economic ties, by raising the standard of living of underdeveloped countries and . . . oh my God, I don't know what all and couldn't list it if I did. It is all, as anyone can see, wholly laudable. And I wouldn't mind any of these activities if the quality of the attention he gave me was the same as he gives to any one of those projects.

It's not so much that I want more of his time, I'd hate a man hanging around the house. It's that I want to be counted as something important. Not the most important, just important. And not just as that warm-body-in-bed.

But it is as if I didn't really exist for him. I am not there (or here) except as an adjunct to the kind of necessary things people do, sleep, eat, socialize. I am here for the housekeeping and food-preparing, I am here for entertaining people and I am here to sleep with. That's all. He does not even know my name.

I will cite the most recent evidence and then I will rest my case.

He and I have planned to go to an island in the Caribbean, one that isn't popular, for 4 or 5 days in Jan. And I have had this vision of us off by ourselves in a cottage on a deserted beach and I have kept this dangling before me like a beautiful carrot ever since Aug. when we talked about it and made the reservations.

Last night, coming back from the Mastersons' (another of their dull, but this time not lethally so, dinners), I spoke to J. of my worry about Ames; how I don't know what she's doing or thinking and how I think she's not happy. J. sort of turned this over in his mind and then he came up with this really wonderful idea, this truly extraordinary inspiration: We Could Take Her Along with Us to the Island.

I almost opened the car door and let myself drop out. Actually, I felt as if he had done just that. The picture of the three of us rose before me: Ames on a bed in the liv. rm; J. Ames and I a cozy threesome in each other's laps, in the cottage, on the beach, all day and all night. Like an old-timey children's book: Honey Bunch on Vacation with Bob and Betty at the Island.

I finally said feebly that Ames would be in school but J. said heartily that a few days out wouldn't matter.

When we got home I sat myself in front of the TV. He went into his study and after a bit he came out and said, It's getting late. Why don't you go to bed?

I said I had things to think about. He didn't say anything, just went on up. He never says anything and he is always going on up, transported into a higher sphere, no doubt.

If he'd asked me what I had to think about, I would've told him. I *wanted* to tell him but the flat-headedness of his asking me why I didn't go to bed made me realize it would be hopeless.

I sat staring at the TV, not hearing it because the sound was off and not seeing it because I was seeing all my hopes crushed as if by a bulldozer.

And it seems to me that that is just what it is like with J. He comes along with his bulldozer and runs over my house, only one mangled rickety bed escaping his Infernal Machine. And I am sitting on the ground looking at the ruins when he comes back and says, It's getting late. Why don't you go to bed?

When I think of how much I had been counting on those four days! There we would be (I thought) on this beautiful sunlit beach, warm and happy and alone. We would swim and walk and return to our cottage to eat and talk and have interc. . . . not just at night (maybe *never* at night) but before lunch and after lunch and not only in bed but maybe on the beach or wherever the fancy struck.

But now, with Ames, we would be a couple of aged parents vacationing in the worst kind of American Togetherness. We would talk and act just as we do here and interc. would be at night only and undoubtedly the beds would squeak and the walls would be made of tissue paper and the whole thing would be as romantic as a Boy Scout Camp.

Of course I could tell him that I do not want to take Ames but what is the point? If he could think of such a thing there is no use in going at all. He would probably rent himself a deep sea diver's oufit and spend all his time incommunicado on the floor of the ocean.

When I finally did go to bed I couldn't sleep. And I couldn't read either. I tried all of the books I just got from the library but even the new one on Shackleton was no help. I did not feel inspired by his heroic efforts on the ice floes, nor on the boat trip to Elephant Island, nor even on the great voyage in the *James Caird,* though I leafed through, trying them all. I felt, in fact, worse, as if I were sitting all alone on the ice floe, watching the *James Caird* disappearing in the fog, knowing it would never return for me.

No use to say any of this to J. He would say I am over-emotional and why don't I tell AB about it. AB in his turn would say I am over-reacting and why don't I tell J. about it. Up the wall with both of them.

Wednesday, Nov. 12

This last week everything (at the Center and most everywhere else) has been planning for Moratorium Day. Last month's march was good but nothing world-shaking. This time it is to be in Washington and everybody is hoping it will shake the world . . . or at least that part of it inhabited by Nixon-Agnew and Co.

Everybody at the Center is going; many of them on early buses that will get there in time for the Death March. That starts Friday night (I think) at Arlington Cemetery and goes past the W. House where the marchers will read names of Vietnam War Dead. The Big March starts Sat. A.M. and goes from the Capitol to the Washington Monument.

Marcia and Tom (two decrepit old kids at the Center . . . they are nearly thirty) are going on a Fri. night bus and tried to persuade me to go with them. I wish I could but I can't. I went to the first Great March, the Martin Luther King one, on a bus but that was a long time ago and I was a lot younger and even then I was dead afterwards. No, I'll go down on the plane and come back that night the way I did for the Poor People's March.

I expect Gabriel will drive down with Vern. I *know* he'll go. He said the other day that he doesn't think this march will do any good but if he didn't go he'd feel he had personally doomed it.

Which is almost exactly my own feeling. And reminds me of the so very dissimilar feelings expressed tonight at dinner. Especially by Ames's new friend. I was in the kitchen getting dinner when she came in with him. She mumbled his name, Jackie something, and said they just wanted to pick up a sandwich and hurry to the seminar (this is the thing on black history).

Ames hasn't had a boy, or indeed any friend but Gretchie around in a long time so I was pleased to see this Jackie. Of course I did notice that he was black and of course my mind did leap to the distant future and I wondered how difficult a black-and-white marriage would be in that future. But that was just normal mother-worrying and I rolled out the Red Carpet and said we were having an early dinner because J. had to get to a meeting so why didn't they stay.

Ames said No thanks, they didn't have time. But Jackie pulled her back, saying they had plenty of time and he'd like to stay, if I really meant it.

I said I did of course.

Then Ames, looking miserable (the poor child obviously did not want us to give her new friend the once-over) said they should be at the seminar well before eight and they didn't have time.

But Jackie said as smoothly as you please that the seminar didn't start till eight-fifteen and they REELY had plenty of time, unless of course Ames had some other reason for not wanting to stay?

And he left it there with the sly innuendo hanging out . . . or so I felt . . . that maybe she was ashamed of him.

And I do not think that feeling was all in my mind because poor Ames blushed and said, Oh, no, no. Sure, if you want to. I mean, OK.

I at once mentally rerolled the Red Carpet. I did not like the way he maneuvered her into staying, the way he exposed her little lie (if it even was one) of the time, and that last thing which seemed to suggest she was ashamed of him was nasty. Nasty and smooth. He made me think of an international jewel thief in a low-cost movie.

The conversation at the table was about M. Day. J. (who is not going, of course) said the March was fine for those who wanted to do it for themselves but he thought it would have no effect at all, unless there were violence. In which case it would give impetus to the Admnstrn's Law and Order stance.

The Jewel Thief couldn't have agreed more, saying he was afraid the marchers' hearts were where their heads ought to be. Which sounded to me like something he cribbed from some lousy columnist, maybe Willie Buckley (I am getting so I can't keep a civil tongue in my head. Just shows what a bad effect hanging around draft-age kids can have on the aged).

Then J. asked Ames if she were going and she said she wasn't.

J. asked her why she didn't go along and keep her mother company.

Raffles looked momentarily startled out of his urbanity and asked if I were REELY going.

J. said they couldn't have marches without me; that I had started marching in the cradle.

So then the Jewel Thief put on an impressed look and said he thought it was great of me. Like if more of you older people (he said) would participate, it would do more good than all the kids.

It looked to me as if he were trying to work both sides of the street so I asked him which side he was on, pro or con the march?

He's on both because while he doesn't want to like march, he does want to like *participate*. He said their school would be open Fri. and Sat. for various activities for people who want to serve (his word) but not march. He is "in charge" of posting notices on the Bulletin Board. Big Deal.

I asked Ames if she were involved in anything and old Raffles jumped right in. Said Ames had organized this great thing for Friday night and all day Sat., a child-care center at the school for parents (in or out of the school) who wanted to march but had no place to leave their kids.

J. prodded Ames for more details but she sat there with her face practically in her plate and said she hadn't organized it and there wasn't anything to tell.

Jackie jumped in again and said some of the teachers would be there and some parents were helping by bringing food, playpens, cribs and stuff.

I said I'd like to help and asked Ames what was needed.

Jackie said there was a list and he'd be glad to drop one off for me. No trouble, no trouble at all.

I did not like that boy and after they all left and I was stacking the d.washer, I felt depressed about him. Then I had to laugh at myself. How my heart had leapt up when I beheld him like a rainbow in the sky, and how now he seemed to me a perfect Crock. Nobody can say I don't have an open mind: Sir Galahad one minute and Shit-Head the next. I have to remember there will be a lot of Crocks in Ames's life and if I get uptight about all of them I'll end in the Funny Farm sooner rather than the later I'd counted on.

I got to wondering what my noodle-headed son and his noodle-headed school were doing about M Day so I called him. He hates us to telephone him so he said he was in the Biggest Rush of His Entire Life and he couldn't talk but one minute. For a miracle, there are buses going from That School and for another miracle, David will be on one of them.

We had a bad connection (is there any other kind these days?) so I had to shout, I thought you didn't approve of things like this. He shouted back that he didn't know what I was talking about; that the March is Participatory Democracy (how that boy does love slogans) and that he and several of the teachers thought it was important that there be no violence so he and they had organized this marshals' group to keep order.

I liked the way he spoke of "me and these teachers" who were clearly in his mind just trailing along in his wake. So different from Ames, who very likely did start the child-care business and now disclaims all responsibility. Still, he is a good boy and there is hope for him so I shouted enthusiastically that I would salute as I passed him in the line.

He almost screamed, My God, you're not going!

I laughed and said, You bet your boots I am.

Then he shouted that he positively HAD to go and with desperate seriousness he added, Don't try to speak to me on Sat. Marshals are not allowed to talk!

I felt restored after that. David is a good, good boy. One of his most endearing traits is this fierce independence which he always had. I think part of the reason he takes such a conservative stand when talking to me is to prove that nothing I have ever thought or said has had the slightest effect on him, that he has raised himself by his own intellectual bootstraps. Which, in a way, he has. I am very proud of that child but of course I have to be very careful about telling him so.

When David hung up, I sat down to catch up on the news: last Sunday's News of the Week in Review, the Wall St. Journal, and some I. F. Stone. And as I went through them I got more and more angry. The attempts by the Admnstrn to frighten people away from this March are worse than I'd realized. They are making these prophecies of violence and blood in the streets. They talk of thousands of National Guard, of troops, of Mace, tear gas and guns. They say no law-abiding citizens will come.

Finally I threw the papers down in an absolute rage. Which comes back to me all over again as I write this. Who the hell do those jerks . . . Nixon, Agnew, Mitchell & Co. . . . think they are telling us to keep off the streets of Washington, D.C.? By God, I'd go if I had to ride the whole way in a crowded subway.

And I got to wondering if other people were as angry as I . . . or if maybe some had been turned off by all this scare talk so I decided to call around and see what people were doing.

It took all evening to reach even a few people but the results were encouraging. Friends like Bill Q. who is much more interested in his greenhouse than the White House was so infuriated by Nixon's Nov. 3rd speech that he is taking the bus at Freedom Square. Polly and Ken are driving down with their two kids. The Gersons are both going (I thought she might but I know he voted for Nixon . . . he said he had never felt so betrayed in his life).

And then it got too late to call any more people here but it occurred to me it was just the right time to call Cissy and see what she was doing.

She answered and when I asked what the plans were out there for Saturday, she came down on me like a ton of bricks.

Plans!!?? she said. What plans? My God, you'd think it was Xmas to hear you. Don't you know all this is serious? Don't you know these kids are killing themselves with pot and drugs and God knows where it'll end? Plans! What the hell kind of plans would I have for Saturday? What the hell do I care about Saturday?

Actually she said more than that. It was clear something awful had happened and when she told me what it was I understood why she was so violent. Little Sophie was arrested some days ago at a pot party, only Sophie was on LSD and by the time they got her out on bail she had to be put in the hospital where she is now.

I poured out sympathy and I asked if Alex was being any help or was he still in the Godhead?

She said that the ghastly business had had one good effect: Alex had thrown out the bell ringers, and shaved off the beard. Only (she said) he has now returned to the church.

Church? I said. What church?

The one and only True Church, she said. Of course he hasn't been a Catholic or anything else in all the 20 very odd years I've known him but he flies from one extreme to another, the same crazy way you do.

Ordinarily when Cissy lashes out with her sharp tongue (and it can be very sharp sometimes), I give it right back to her. But this time I figured she was entitled to lash and I just said I would be glad to go stay with her if she wanted me to. She said there was nothing I could do right now but she'd yell if she needed me.

Tomorrow I am going to have 2 or 3 dozen anemones wired to her. She will make a wry face when she sees them but they'll cheer her up. She has always said she has never had enough anemones. Maybe it should be 4 doz.

Later when I was getting ready for bed, Deb called. She was in a bad state. Partly it was because she'd been drinking. But the fact is that her life *is* hard and bleak. Struggling to keep up with her classes (at the Social Work school), to take care of the 3 kids, to manage on very little money and never to have anything . . . even the simplest kind of pleasure . . . for herself. At one point, I got so worried that I offered to come over and spend the night. But after we'd talked awhile she said she felt enough better to sleep.

We're meeting for lunch tomorrow and I think I'll mention a new Women's Lib group I heard about (I would go myself if the Counseling Center didn't keep me so busy that I hardly have time to get food into the house). Of course what Deb *wants* is a man. And I am still looking for one for her but there just aren't any. What a wicked world it is where any old toothless, beat-up bore of a man can find some woman (and often a pretty nice one) and even the most attractive, intelligent females, if they are over 35, find themselves sitting alone with the late-night movie night after night after night.

Friday, Nov. 14

Briefly at the Center today where everything was organized pandemonium as people got themselves squared away for rides and buses.

Gabriel is driving down with Sam and some others in Vern's car and Gabriel said why didn't I come too. We can squeeze you in somewhere, he said.

Of course I wouldn't go with them but the remark made me feel as extraneous as an old mattress they might tie on the top. But then, later, he said we should meet for lunch and we agreed to be at the base of the Monument at one o'clock. Everybody is taking food and Gabriel warned me to wear "long drawers" against the cold ground. I felt better after that, not so left-out and antiquated.

Now I am here in the kitchen, writing this. Having washed my thermals I am listening to them roaring away in the dryer and waiting for Ames. I am going to drive her to school with some stuff we have collected for the nursery business.

Oh, I pray that Washington will be jammed with people tomorrow and that all of us will be as meek and mild as Jesus's little lambs.

Saturday, Nov. 15

It's late Sat. night and I went and I am back.

I was up early and out of the house before J. was awake. Left the car at the airport and caught the plane. Good thing I reserved last week, there were a lot of stand-bys and the plane was full.

In Washington, waiting for a cab, I got to talking to a nice, elderly (probably about 2 yrs. older than I) black man who was also going to the March so we shared a cab. He was Hibbard Larkins, Master Plumber (he gave me his card), now living in some little town in the boondocks outside Boston, formerly of Grand Cayman, B.W.I. He had a slight and very nice accent . . . Scotch I thought and it turned out it was. G.C. was settled, he told me, by Scots seamen. He had been to the Freedom March (that seems so long ago as to have been another geological era) and we talked about that and agreed that nothing would ever be like that again. Then we were at the Capitol and we got out and tried to find out where the line was.

At first there didn't seem to be any line, just thousands and thousands of people milling about . . . pouring into the plaza from all the surrounding streets. Finally, after we prowled around, we found the line on Pa. Ave. and we got into it and it was, as the kids say, like tremendous.

The line, about ten people wide, stretched as far as one could see, and from all the side streets people were pouring down and joining in. The line was on one side of the Ave. . . . it was forbidden to go into the middle of the street . . . and marshals stood along on the outside of the line (facing the marchers) at intervals of about 3 feet to keep people in line. They (the marshals) were all kids and they were absolutely great. It was cold, colder than Washington has any right to be, and some of the kids had no gloves or mittens, almost none of them were warmly dressed and yet they smiled and said, THINK WARM and they held out boxes of tissues for dripping noses.

Then, as we walked along, I saw David. He was behind the marshals, handing them cups from a carton he was carrying. As we came up to him, I called out, Hi, David! Then, as soon as he saw me, I said, How's your mother?

He did a double take and then he grinned and said, She's just fine.

As we passed on, Hibbard said, That was a handsome boy. And I took great pleasure in saying that his parents are the salt of the earth.

It was a clear day but the sun kept going in and out and we were on the shady side of the street and there was a bitter wind. By the time we rounded the corner, at 15th St., I was thanking God and Gabriel for the long drawers and my last-minute decision to wear ski pants.

There at 15th St. we saw the buses . . . great lines of Capitol Transit (and other) buses parked bumper to bumper against the curb. At first I thought they must have brought people to the March but somebody said (rightly, I later learned) that they were parked like that all around, forming a wall around the White House area. Nixon's cordon sanitaire.

What kind of mentality does he have to react to

this peaceful expression of opinion by retreating behind a fortress of buses . . . that he refuses even to listen ("under no circumstances will I be affected by it whatsoever")? I fail utterly to understand what manner of man he is. The thing is that I cannot believe he *is* a man. He is like some battery-operated toy man that you'd get at FAO Schwartz (and return right away because there's something wrong with it).

Pig-Face Agnew with his turgid tirades ("the strident minority who raise intolerant clamor and cacophony") is much easier. The Fat-Boy, slowest in the class, meanest on the playground, jealous of money, position and intelligence. At last he has the dough and the position and armed with a dictionary and an 1898 edition of "Elegant Rhetoric for the Platform Speaker" he is telling the Bright Boys where to head in.

I read later that Nixon spent the day watching some football game on TV.

Anyway, we were out there in the street and as we passed the mall on our left we could see another huge army coming up it, people who had not been able to get into this line and so had formed another.

When we got to the Monument, people scattered, most of them going down the hill towards the Reflecting Pool, near the speakers' stand. Hibbard (he kept telling me to call him Hibbie but somehow I never did) and I went to look for toilets which we finally found. They were portables like at the other marches only not nearly so many. We saw only 2 sets of 6 booths.

Then, back up to the Monument where I told Hibbard we had to wait for some people with whom we'd have lunch. He protested that he wanted to take me out to lunch which was perfectly silly. As I told him, it would take hours and we'd miss the speakers and, anyway, I wanted to be where the action was.

I didn't tell him that I also wanted to see Gabriel. I was surprised and even a little alarmed at how much I did want to see him. Good God, I said to myself, have I turned into an old female roué, like Mrs. Robinson in "The Graduate"? I tried to think that my feelings were just friendly but I couldn't kid myself. There we were, Hibbard and I, bent against this really searing wind, circling around and around the Monument because I had to see Gabriel. It wasn't friendship that was driving me to freeze my very bones.

Anyway, we kept on circling and I kept on looking, getting more and more frantic, until Hibbard plucked at my sleeve and said, Your friends aren't coming, Sophie. There's just too many people and they couldn't make it.

And finally reason asserted itself and I realized Hibbard was right. So we worked our way down the hill and staked out a claim to a little 2 ft. square piece of earth and sat down on it and listened to the speakers and the singers.

After a while Hibbard and I ate, sharing our lunches, a lopsided sharing since Hibbard had beautiful-looking sandwiches, carrot sticks, a thermos of coffee and pound cake which he said his wife made. I had Swiss cheese between two pieces of dry bread, an apple and some Slim Jim sticks. Which Hibbard took a great liking to so I gave him those in exchange for coffee and lb. cake.

It was terribly cold sitting there, the sun wasn't out much and the wind was icy but I got annoyed at Hibbard's solicitude. He kept saying how cold I must be and trying to make me sit on his carryall. Of course

I was cold but so was he and I had my own carryall and there was something wrong about his fussing over me as if I were the Princess who slept on a pea.

Then, somewhere along in the middle, Pete Seeger sang and asked everybody to sing with him: All we are saying is give peace a chance. And everybody did. We all stood with hands raised in the V, all singing. And Pete would say, Sing it louder, so they can hear it in the White House. Louder so they can hear it in Vietnam. And the voices got louder and louder . . . ALL WE ARE SAYING IS GIVE PEACE A CHANCE (I hear it in my head right now). And the whole wonderful happening moved me, moved me as We Shall Overcome had done when we sang it on Freedom March Day. And when we stopped, my eyes and nose were running and I kissed Hibbard on both cheeks.

I think he looked stunned but I couldn't see too well. Then we sat back down and there was more (Coretta King was very good) but the Great Time for me was that whole-souled singing. And then suddenly it was all over.

Hibbard wanted us to go somewhere for a drink but it was cold (somehow I felt Washington getting colder and more sinister-seeming now that we were dispersing) and it was all over and I wanted to get home. So we went to the Ave. and a policeman told us where we'd likely get a cab and we went there and we did.

At the airport Hibbard decided to change his ticket from a later plane to my earlier one, which somehow annoyed me. I didn't know why at the time. I thought it was because I was tired and wanted to be by myself.

Anyway, while he was doing that I got a hot dog and read the Wash. Star which estimated the crowd at

500,000. Later, some reports lowered the number to 250,000. I'll bet anything there were at least 6 or 7 hundred thousand, maybe even, as one speaker said, a million. But no one will ever know. The army helicopters that were buzzing overhead could say, but of course they will not.

It was on the plane that I began to get what was to be my great *éclair* about Hibbard and me. And Gabriel and me. Hibbard ordered drinks right off. A double Scotch, he said, and then in a very expansive way he said to me, Have anything you want. The sky's the limit.

There seemed something vaguely like an old-fashioned Sugar Daddy in his attitude which I didn't much like. I ordered a Gibson and as soon as the drinks came, he ordered another double for himself and tried (without success) to force another Gibson on me.

Then he got to talking about The Movement (whatever that means to him) and he was back there on the steps of the Memorial, quoting at length from the I Had a Dream Speech (it seemed so terribly long ago, in a better, more hopeful time, that it made me sad) and then he said he would tell me why he was in The Movement. It was a piece of information I could have lived without but of course there was no avoiding it.

I begin (he said) with Jesus of Nazareth who said he died for me. And if his death brought life to me then I must share my inheritance with my brothers.

He went on and on about Jesus and brotherhood and life after death and I thought he was building up to something, some one statement that would draw it all together but if he did I missed it because suddenly he was leaning back and saying. And that, Sophie, is why I am in The Movement.

Then he beamed at me and said he could see I was a Believer too.

It wasn't easy to be respectful of his beliefs (whatever they were) and still convince him that I had none similar to his, or even any that were sufficiently concrete to tell him. He maintained to the last that I would one day go with him to his church in Grand Cayman (where he goes sometimes to visit his old mother). And it was when he began talking about this that I got very definitely uncomfortable.

He put his hand on my arm and spoke of all he would do for me (in G.C.), the feast his ancient mother would prepare, how he would carry me from one end of the island to the other "to show you off, a rare woman like you, little Sophie" (*little* Sophie!). You are my kind of woman, he said. Then he gave me a meaningful, sort of soulful leer (I *think* it was a leer) and said, I saw it when first you took up with me and I saw it when you bestowed your smile on me and I saw it again when you kissed me.

And that is when the first 300-watt light burst on me.

To me, the "taking up" with him was just ordinary, everyday life. I would've taken up with anybody who happened to be going my way just as I would've given the same runny-nosed, runny-eyed kiss to anybody I had shared the experience with. The whole friendly day was just that to me and I didn't care if I ever saw Hibbard again. I liked him, but for this one day and that was all.

But to Hibbard a "rare" (whatever that meant, it meant something) woman like me would not take up with a man like him (meaning, I must suppose, his color) and kiss him, however casually, and share sandwiches and cabs if it didn't mean something. He thought something special had happened to me (and I suppose he might have kidded himself into thinking it had happened to him also) and not only had I bestowed my smile on him but I was ready to bestow other favors as well. (My God, I'm beginning to sound like him.)

So I had to set myself to straighten things out . . . in a way that wouldn't let him down. I said how wonderful it would be to go to his island and how my husband and all (*sic*) my children would like it and I asked if he took his family with him when he went (I knew he had a wife on account of the lb. cake).

At first he didn't much want to talk about the family but gradually he warmed up and finally he pulled out his wallet and showed me pictures of them . . . Hibbard Jr. studying for the ministry, Clementine with three little girls, and Sharleen, a beauty with a wide grin and braids with bows on them.

I praised each one and then I asked if he did not have any pictures of his wife.

He said no, that she did not hold with graven images.

That struck me with all the ambiguities in it (did she think it blasphemous to have any pictures at all? If so, why these of her children? Or did she think *she* was an idol or that she would become one if photographed?) that I didn't get the beginning of Hibbard's discourse. When I tuned in again he was off on his church (it is world-wide and he has friends everywhere); his business (he has put installations in the best homes and factories and if I ever need anything . . . even a washer changed . . . I'm to call and he will come running).

Finally the plane landed and we parted. That went all right . . . we had already exchanged telephone numbers and promises to meet for the next march if there is another. I got the car from the parking lot and came home.

It wasn't late when I came in. J. was working at his desk but Ames was asleep, having spent (J. said) an exhausing 24 hours with 18 small children.

He seemed interested in how the day had been so I told him about it and about David and the Capitol Transit Fortress and, of course, about Hibbard.

Anytime you want to go to Grand Cayman (I said), you just say the word and Hibbard will put out the welcome mat.

For you, J. said. I doubt his welcome would include me.

I'm sure any friend of mine is a friend of his, I said.

I doubt it, J. said in the ½ ironic–½ amused way he has. I think you made a conquest there.

Hey, I did, didn't I? And for a minute I sat there grinning. Then as I thought about it, I said, But I really don't understand why he fell on me . . . not literally of course . . . but just assumed I would be delighted to go down life's pathway with him. I mean, even if he has backward ideas about a white woman being friendly to a black man.

I suppose that's it in part, J. said. But the other and more important part is the way you are.

What way am I? I said, not angry just puzzled.

Oh, you know how you are. You *must* know, he said, laughing. You go overboard with a kind of friendliness that could easily be confused with something else, especially by somebody like your friend Hibbard, who is already somewhat confused about what role he is supposed to play.

You trying to say I lead people on? That I'm like what we used to call a tease?

Something like that, he said. Then he smiled and said, I'm sure you don't mean to be. But you do seem to promise more than you deliver.

But I'm only being friendly! I said.

You seem to be quite ready to give people the shirt off your back, J. said. To strangers . . . to people who hardly know you . . . this can seem like something more than friendliness.

Well! I said. I guess I'd better mend my ways or I'm liable to end up in the poky for soliciting.

It's funny, J. said, but you don't do it with people you know. At least, I've never noticed it. But you do act that way with comparative strangers like your Hibbard.

It's funny, I said. But I'm not laughing. I must be an absolute dope, a real fathead to go around with WELCOME printed in scarlet letters on my forehead.

It would be nice, J. said, if you wore those letters at home.

I stared at him for a minute and then suddenly I was so embarrassed I couldn't look at him. The thing of it is, he never says anything like that. And I'm just not used to his being a man who notices me as a female in broad 75-watt light. So I quickly got up and eased myself out of the room.

Later (and not much later) he came to bed where I was reading and of course I knew there was no turning off this conquest. So I accepted it with all good intentions. But the road to great interc. is not, I guess, paved with good intentions. I suppose it was pretty unrewarding for him too but who would ever know? He keeps his lip buttoned up as tightly in bed as out of it. Our talk tonight was the longest and most friendly one we've had since I can remember. Maybe if it had been longer and more friendly the interc. would have been better?

I couldn't sleep afterwards so I came in here to the guest room. I wanted to write but I also wanted to think. I can read when J. is sleeping but I can't think. Somehow his breathing makes me feel he can overhear my private thoughts.

And the thoughts tonight are about Gabriel and myself. It was seeing how Hibbard had gone so wrong about me that made me realize I have done the same thing with Gabriel as Hibbard did with me. And now, with J.'s words about my seeming to promise more than I will deliver, it falls into an all too clear pattern.

My meeting with Gabriel has seemed to me a special event and his "taking up" with me even more special. I have thought that his friendliness for somebody like me (me being old and thus inferior, as Hibbard thought that *he* was because of his color), must mean that Gabriel also saw our meeting as special. But when I add the fact that I go overboard, as J. says I do, in my attempts at friendliness, then it becomes obvious that Gabriel is only reacting in a normal, friendly way to my friendliness. He would have been equally kind and friendly to anybody else except he would probably not have expressed the friendliness so openly had I not seemed to invite it. All the feeling that I have worked up for him is in *my* head, not his.

It is, I suppose, understandable that "a woman like

me" aging, lorn and lonely would try to fill the emptiness with whatever came to hand. But understandable or not, I am disgusted with myself. I feel as if I had tried to be a heroine in a bad, bad movie, one of those things with Lana Turner as the Older Woman, all cotton-candy hair and easy, greasy tears at the renunciation scene. Well, I don't have cotton-candy hair and there'll be no renunciation scene since there is nothing to renounce but my besotted fancies.

What a day this has been. A great day in some ways and a sad one in others. And not because I see that I am not Gabriel's special old lady friend but just his old lady friend. But sad because I have the strongest conviction that this March will be the last thing of its kind. Today when it was over and the helicopters droned overhead and the wind blew and the sky darkened and people started straggling off, I felt like crying out to them, Don't go! It's our last chance to be together. The Ice Age is coming.

Saturday, Nov. 22

I am slumped down here at the table in the kitchen and I don't think my bones will ever rise again.

J. just left to catch the early shuttle to NY. Went down to see the Foundation people again. Still trying to get some money for one of his ghetto projects and they still looking at it, and him, with deepest suspicion as if he were going to take the $$ and run. He is ever persevering, too noble by half.

And too far above the battle for me. Just now, before

he left, I was sitting here all broken down, reading about the My Lai Massacre. I feel such a sickness I wish I could vomit it up. I said something about it to J. as he stood here knocking back a cup of coffee.

J. agreed it is appalling (I must admit he did look grim). But why (he said) must you keep on reading it? It will make you sicker and doesn't do anybody any good.

I said I had to read it.

He said, You don't need to read every horrible detail. It's not (he said) as if we didn't already know that atrocities are being committed there. Daniel Lang's thing in the NYker about that gang rape, you remember.

I said not to remind me, that it was as real to me as if I had been the girl's mother.

But, J. said, you see *everything* that way. There's no need of it and no purpose is served by it.

It is hopeless to tell him that this isn't something I *want* to do; that I try hard to back off but I don't seem able to. So I shut my mouth and kept on reading but then as I came to yet another blood-chilling detail I groaned and said, Oh my God, how wonderful we are to bring our civilization to these poor, backward people!

J. said, You really must stop that.

Oh, leave me alone, I snarled.

He sighed and said he wished he could do something to help me. Then he sighed again and said he wished that psychiatrist could do something for me.

I mentally curled my lip at the thought of AB. The other day I asked him to write letters to our senators (it doesn't matter for what, it was important) and he wanted to know why I felt the need to involve him in my concerns. MY concerns!

J. finished his coffee and gathered up his things and I wished him luck with the Money Bags and then I came back and slumped down here.

I did put the papers away. J. is right . . . it doesn't do any good and is, as he would say, counter-productive since it so enfeebles me I don't even feel up to writing to Brooke, Kennedy, and Fat-Face Nixon.

I am going to shut this damn notebook and go stand on my head and get the hell out of here.

Sunday, Nov. 23

Yesterday I tried to make myself do some errands at the Square but I kept seeing those dead bodies, the children with their little legs all askew, and hearing (and seeing) our brave boys saying "Let's see what she's made of" as they tore the clothes off a 13-yr.-old girl. I could not do anything except wander around, finally ending in the Booksmith where I stood staring at the New Books table.

And that is what I was doing when I felt a hand on my shoulder and I turned to see Gabriel. I was so glad to see him I almost wept. It's odd because he's not even an old friend, but just seeing him made me feel there is hope for something, if not the human race, maybe dolphins or birds or bats. I would settle for anything except cockroaches, which, I'm sure, already have a Spiro T. and a Richard M.

And I said, Oh, I AM glad to see you.

Right away he said, Is something wrong?

I said no and he asked if I had time for coffee so we went next door to the cafeteria.

As we were sitting with our coffees, he asked again what was the matter. You look (he said) like you lost your last friend.

I said it was My Lai, that I couldn't get it out of my mind.

His face all clouded up as he said, Those bastards, those mother-fucking bastards.

It wasn't just fucking, I said, And it wasn't just mothers. And then suddenly as if they had just been waiting for the chance to come out, the tears gushed out of my eyes.

I said I was sorry and I wiped my eyes with a napkin and I drank some coffee.

Why shouldn't you cry? he said. Shows you're human.

And he handed me another napkin to blow my nose in. Finish your coffee, he said. And we'll go walk some.

We went out and walked up towards the Square. I was so cold . . . I had been cold all morning and now I got colder. It was partly because I am still wearing my fall coat. I have not got the fur one out of storage because I am ashamed to wear it. It is not one of the furs on the endangered list and sheared beaver is actually not even an expensive fur. But still I am ashamed of it. It is so Establishment-looking, like a card of identity saying "Upper Middle Class."

But I was also cold, I think, because the world seemed barren and hostile and cold. And as we walked I started to shiver.

Gabriel still had his arm sort of linked through mine and he said, Baby, you got the shakes.

Just then we were at the corner by the First Church and he said, Let's duck in here and warm you up.

So we went in and looked around. There were some white flowers at the altar and it was full of peaceful warmth. Nobody was there but it did not feel empty, only full of quietness.

Gabriel went over to one of the family pews along the side, the ones that have half-fences around them, and he said, Let's sit here.

So we sat on the cushioned seats in our own little enclosure and he said, I like this church. Puts me in mind of my Daddy's. His wasn't so fancy in some ways, no cushions for example, but we had a lot of pretty stained glass these cats don't have.

I asked him if he had ever wanted to be a minister. He was sitting forward with his elbows on his knees, the way he often sits, looking at his hands (he has the longest, leanest fingers I have ever seen). And he said, No. And then he laughed.

You know what I wanted to be? he said. A cowboy in a Wild West show.

I started to ask what was funny and then I stopped and said, You mean the color wouldn't do?

He looked at me with a look that was . . . what? . . . amused, kindly, and something else, something so close, so accepting that I felt as if I were ten yrs. old and he was my good 12-yr.-old cousin Henry, pointing out to me in a cousinly way some dumb thing I had said.

And feeling that family closeness I put one hand on both of his and I said, I'm sorry. You ought to be able to be a cowboy. Everybody ought to be able to be a cowboy.

Everybody ought to be able to be president, he said. But, Sis, you and me, we got no chance at all of being cowboys nor presidents.

We got it tough, I said smiling too. Then I thought

of My Lai and my smile vanished and I said, But the Vietnamese have got it the toughest of all.

He patted my shoulder and stood up. Let's go to the ice cream parlor and get us some soul food, he said.

Then as we went out of our pew, he put his arm around my shoulders and said, Cheer up, girl. Anybody human has got it tough these days.

We went and got our cones and then he had a class and I came on home.

I don't exactly know why I feel better (I felt enough improved to write B., K., and Fat-Face). Nothing is any different. I suppose it is just being with an understanding human being.

It finally dawns on me what it really is between Gabriel and me: we are like what he calls kinfolk. For whatever reason, we seem to have a kind of family closeness.

Monday, Nov. 24

What a Thanksgiving this is going to be.

I ordered the foreign student some time ago and today they called to say I am the lucky winner of somebody named, I think, Mekong Delta. He comes from Taiwan which is not my favorite place in this world. I'd told them I'd take anybody nobody else wanted but now, of course, I hope that's not what I got.

I have asked Deb because her children are going to Marsden (she'll have them for Xmas) and J.'s brother, who just got his divorce, is coming up. I would be hoping that something would happen between him and Deb except he is an all-wool, yard-wide Repub. (I think he voted for Goldwater and I know he voted for Nixon). David hasn't yet said if he's bringing anybody but I suppose he's coming. Ames hasn't said anything and I keep hoping she'll tell me whether she'll be here before I have to ask her.

Gabriel is going to Vern's place. The other day he asked me if I would go with him. I told him I couldn't and about the people who are coming here and then we imagined what it would be like if we could transport these people to Vern's, and as we pictured Deb and my Establishment brother-in-law using the facilities (the nearest . . . or furthest . . . tree) and those two and Mekong Delta in sleeping bags and making up dialogue for them, we got to laughing and I turned over a paint can.

We are painting his room. I don't know whose idea it was. Like a lot of things we think of, it seems as if we thought of it simultaneously. I know I had been thinking . . . just sort of on the periphery of my mind . . . of how I would like to do something about the dirty beige walls and from time to time I would pick at the chipping paint with my fingernail, and then one day he came home with a putty knife and started scraping off the badly chipping part. And we said, Why don't we just go ahead and do it?

For some time now, I have been going there to type up his notes (it takes him a year to type a page). Now I go early and type awhile and then I paint until it's time to go to the Center. It is going to be a nice soft gray when it is finished.

I like that room, I always feel warm and comfortable in it. It's small but it's nice and light. It has one long window high up on the wall over the couch-bed and when there is any sun (as there seems to have been lately) it pours in.

A few days ago when Gabriel and I were going home (to his room, that is) we met Milton Simms (a colleague of J.'s) on the street. I introduced them and said Gabriel and I work together at the Center. And afterwards I was thinking how I lead these two lives, the wife-mother one who knows people like Milton Simms and the other one who works at the Center and is friends with Gabriel. And like What's His Name who was an FBI man posing as a Communist, my lives are wholly separate. Gabriel knows about the other life but he has never seen it and they not only have never seen him but don't know he exists. I've thought sometimes about having him here to dinner but somehow I like to keep him separate, just for myself.

If I were to be honest (*pathologically* honest) I would have to admit it's because I don't want Gabriel to see me as the middle-class, middle-aged housewife. All right, I do admit it.

Wednesday, Nov. 26

It's all fallen in and I don't give a shit what happens to anybody.

Monday J. told me he was going to England the next day, Tuesday, for some economics meeting and he'll be away all this week. Said he didn't want to go especially as he has to go again right after Xmas to the big London meeting (something I had mercifully forgotten and which enraged me even more). He said he refused when he was first asked but now the delegate is sick and there is nobody to fill in.

Sick! I said. Why, he's probably off in the Caribbean basking in the sun with his wife or somebody and has left you to pick up the pieces.

It turns out the man has had a serious heart attack so I was supposed to feel small and guilty. I did, but not much and not for long. I said I didn't give a damn. I said *I* was about to have a heart attack myself. I said, Shit on those mothering bastards.

At which J. raised an eyebrow and said my language had certainly become more colorful lately.

I said it came from hanging around with kids on street corners. (Actually, the kids at the Center talk that way a lot.) I got no home, I said to him. There's nothing for me to do but hang around on street corners.

He said he was desperately sorry. And he did sound sorry.

And then I thought WHY DON'T I GO TOO?? Mrs. K. could come and do the dinner (the day before if necessary), Deb could be hostess and David and Ames wouldn't give a hoot if I were here or not. So I said, Why don't I go with you?

He said the conference is to be someplace in the country outside London, at some old dungeon it sounded like, and they'll all be living and working there and he was afraid there was no provision for women.

At that my heart dropped and my eyes filled up and I went out to the kitchen to run the water and turn on the disposal so I could beat on the counter and try to rebuild the Stone Wall that usually protects me from disappointments like this. But I kept thinking of J. in Merrie England in a cozy castle (how quickly the dungeon was converted) sitting before a roaring fire with lovely Forsyte Saga People and I felt like The Little Match Girl looking in at the Xmas Feast. One thing I know, I will never again ask him to take me anywhere, anytime, for any reason.

Later I got to feeling outraged that there was to be no provision for women. If there are female secretaries I suppose they will just have to creep out to the copse to crap.

And I wondered if there really is such a thing as penis envy or is it just something males invented to bolster up their egos. I asked old AB about this a while back and he turned it back on me and asked me what I thought.

I said I guessed I didn't think there is such a thing; that I didn't think most women envied men for being men (and having a penis) but for their confidence that being a man is justification enough for existing. A woman usually feels (at least I feel) an ever-present need to demonstrate her right to exist. Of course I never do demonstrate it which is probably what nagging backache, inner tension, Excedrin and Geritol are all about.

Last night I drove J. to the airport, or rather, he drove us. He seems to feel it demeans him if I drive. Maybe a penis isn't much of a security blanket even for those who have it? Driving back I was so sunk, feeling left-out and alone, that I drove right through the toll booth without putting in the quarter. And when the radio played "Sitting on the Dock of the Bay," which Gabriel plays a lot, I started crying and kept on, all the way home.

Later, David called to ask if he could go with his roommate and family to ski in Aspen and of course I said yes. And this morning Ames tells me she is going to the country with Gretchie and the Steins. My cup runneth over.

I called Philadelphia and told Mr. Republican that neither J. nor the children would be here and maybe he'd prefer to make it another time. He said that certainly *would* be best (he doesn't like me much either).

Then I called Deb; told her what the dinner would be and gave her a chance to back out. But she said she would not dream of leaving me in the lurch. Actually, I was hoping that's just where she would leave me. I could take the Mekong Delta alone better than with her. She thinks now she won't mind but when she has a drink or 2 or 3, her paranoia sets in and she's likely to think I arranged everything just to put her down. (As Gabriel would say.)

Speaking of Gabriel, I wonder if I could ask him to come and help me out. The prospect of Deb and Delta is really appalling. Maybe he *would* come. I know Sam is going up to Vern's Thursday night so he could have dinner here in the afternoon and go up afterwards with Sam. I'm going to call him right now.

Sunday, Nov. 30

I don't know how to write this. I just don't know how to. I might as well just write it off the top of my head.

I couldn't get Gabriel on the phone . . . it's in the hall and it's always busy . . . so I went over. He was there with Sam and Harry. At the beginning I wondered what they made of me, but they seemed just to accept me as a friend of Gabriel's from the Center who does his typing so I stopped thinking about it.

We talked some, mostly about the Chicago trial which is a travesty. We were all bitter but Sam was the bitterest, seething. I like Sam but I begin to feel he regards me with suspicion. Must ask Gabriel sometime if this is real or just my paranoia.

Anyway, they left and I told Gabriel about Thanksgiving and asked if he could come and shore me up. He said right off he would. Then he said that as I had nobody to stay home for, I could come up to Vern's with him afterwards. I said I couldn't and that he must not stay if he were doing it with the thought I would go to Vern's because I wouldn't.

He said he wasn't staying for that; that he was staying because I asked him. (When I write this I see what anybody, even such a brain-damaged person as myself, should have seen. But I didn't).

So, by 2 p.m. Thanksgiving Day we four were assembled. Mekong (whose name is really more like Kwai Fong but I am used to the other now) was a short, heavy-set young man with an enormous jaw, little black beetle eyes and a set of pointed teeth which looked like the portcullis of an old castle when he smiled. Kind of scary-looking. He spoke very little English but was fluent in what he said was French.

Deb looked wonderful in a new suit and at first she was very nice to both Mekong and Gabriel but then she got going on the bourbon and by the time we got to the table she wasn't nice anymore.

The dinner was horrid. Pointless, messy and depressing. Deb drank a bottle of wine all by herself and kept proposing toasts in French to which Mekong replied with Fifa La Funtz (he put away the better part of a bottle by himself in addition to the drinks Deb poured down him before dinner). Finally the poor boy couldn't hold his head up and he pushed his pie away and put his head down on the table and snored.

Deb snarled at me and said things like how strange the brother-in-law hadn't materialized and how she never expected to find herself all alone with two teen-age boys on Thanksgiving Day.

I said she wasn't alone; that she still had me, her old pal Sophie. I was trying for the light touch but I might as well have heaved a brick at her. She gave me a really outraged look and said, YOU are the architect of my defeat. (When she's in her cups she often sounds like Winston Churchill.)

Then she got up and went to the pantry to forage for the brandy. A little fine champagne cognac is what's needed, she kept muttering.

Gabriel and I had been exchanging glances off and on during dinner and now we exchanged another, despairing on my part and reassuring on his.

Sophie (he said), you've had it. Give me your car keys and I'll get him home while you see what you can do about her.

I got the keys and then he said to heat up the coffee. He had to get some down old Portcullis who was still out on the table. While I was doing that, Deb came in the kitchen with the brandy bottle and wanted to know where were all the lovely brandy glasses she and Marsden had given us.

I felt like telling her that that was ten years ago and they were all broken. But instead I told her I was sorry

I couldn't ask her to stay but I had to go call on somebody and I was late already.

Deb answered with a quaver in her voice, I never thought I'd see the day.

Usually at that I would've relented but Gabriel was right. I had had it and I walked out of the kitchen with the coffee.

Gabriel had the Yellow Peril propped up and as soon as I poured the coffee, he began getting it past the Portcullis.

Deb came by on her way to the front door and I followed her, saying again I was sorry. She called me a faithless, perfidious ally (Churchill again) and banged out. I was relieved that she had walked. If she hadn't, I would've had to drive her home.

I closed the door then immediately reopened it as Gabriel came up with Delta who was unfocused but ambulatory. I watched Gabriel get him into the car and drive away and then I started clearing the table and stacking the d.washer.

I don't know when I have felt so mean and ugly and so desperate and abandoned. I was at the sink scrubbing the pots when Gabriel came back.

Well, anyway, he said, it was a good dinner.

Was it? I said grimly.

Give me something to dry the pots with, he said.

I picked up the towel and turned around to hand it to him and I looked up at him and he looked back and then he bent and kissed me.

It was a very light kiss but it was as if I had been blessed. All the cold, hard meanness fell off me like cracked plaster.

Let's hurry up and finish these dishes so we can get in the car and go, he said.

He said it perfectly matter-of-factly as if it had long ago been settled that we'd go. And maybe, in some kind of way, it had. Certainly it was now settled.

We finished cleaning up, not talking, and I felt all the time as if I were in a kind of dream. Like somebody in one of those slow-motion TV advertisements, I seemed to be floating along, light in mind and body.

I went up and changed into blue jeans and he said to bring a sleeping bag if I had one so I brought both Ames's and David's. And then we left.

He was driving and almost right away he reached out his right hand and took my left. It didn't occur to me to wonder what I was doing or to think about it at all. It was dark and warm in the car and I fell asleep.

Sometime later I awoke and we were in a lighted drive-in. We had hamburgers and coffee in the car and he said it would be another couple of hours before we got to Vern's. I said I was sorry it would be so long. He said, Maybe we could find a place on the way.

I said, Not a motel. Then he said a road or a field would be fine. I said I was sorry the little car was so little. And he said, Who needs a car when there is all outdoors?

And sometime later we saw a dirt turnoff and drove down it and there was nothing along it and only a clearing at the end. We took out the sleeping bags and he opened one out and then he said, Sophie? Are you all right?

I said I was. And he said, I mean, do you . . .

I said I knew what he meant and I was all right. And then I took my sneakers off and I said, And now I am not a little old lady in white tennis shoes.

Then we took our jeans off and he put the other sleeping bag over us and as I looked up at him, I saw the moon in the sky behind his head and I said, Why, we are in a FIELD. And as he said, Sophie, Sophie, his right hand closed over my left.

Monday, Dec. 1

It is still dark, dawn has not even cracked yet, but I awoke a while ago as if all the alarms in the world had gone off.

Made coffee and walked around, looking out the windows, asking myself, What am I doing?

Now I have come up here and I am still asking, What am I doing?

When I left Gabriel last night we said we'd see each other tomorrow (today) at the Center and I came home in the euphoric state I'd been in all weekend. And, in that same state, I wrote in this notebook and fell into bed.

Now, in the cold, black light of this day, I think I must have been insane. Insane to go off with Gabriel as I did; insane to sleep with him; insane to think we could go on with it. Because that is certainly what I did think last night.

All weekend there at Vern's place, I felt physically and metaphysically transported. And it was not just the sex (actually we only slept together once up there, one day when we were walking in the woods). It was what had been there all along and what the sleeping together only confirmed. Everything seemed right. There were 7 of us, 4 men and 3 girls. Two of the men were black, one of the girls was. But color didn't matter. Nor did age. Vern is early thirties but the others were all as young as or younger than Gabriel. I was the oldest, of course. But that didn't matter either. Or it didn't then.

But now I am back in this house and my 16-year-old daughter is asleep down the hall and day after tomorrow my husband will return and I realize I am an old married woman with all the barnacles that 18 years of marriage brings. How could I have an affair (what else would it be?) with a young man? How could I have an affair at all?

I have never deceived J. about anything and I know I could not do it about something as crucial as this. But, even if I were willing and able to, would I want my children to have a mother sneaking off to have an affair? And with somebody nearer their ages than my own? Even if they didn't know, *I* would know.

And Gabriel, what's in this for him? What good could it do him to hang around with an old married woman? And a white woman at that. I'm sure that at least some of his friends would find me a sinister influence. And maybe I would be. I think I care about his life, his welfare, his good. And that I would never do him any harm. But how do I know what I would do?

I've never been in anything like this before. I don't know what happens or what might happen. I might start clinging to him and he might want to leave me.

I do know I don't want a casual little screwing affair with Gabriel. I don't want an affair period. I want just to be with Gabriel. But that is not possible.

I hear Ames in the shower so I must stop and go down and get breakfast.

And I must stop this whatever-it-is. I will tell him today. But, probably, he has already realized how ridiculous it is for us to be together. Probably he will be relieved that he is not expected to continue with me.

Oh my God, what a terrible wrench those words give me. I feel as if I'd been punched in the stomach.

Monday night

Went late to the Center, and walking home with Gabriel I told him that I knew the weekend had been a temporary aberration and that we couldn't go on with it but I hoped we'd still be friends.

I tried to sound cheerful and casual and I utterly despised myself for the phony manner and the phony words.

Gabriel stopped and looked at me and very grimly he said, You want to tell me those words again? I didn't get them right.

I was embarrassed and ashamed but I tried again, saying, in only slightly different words, the same thing about how we could not go on with this.

He wanted to know what we could not go on with.

And I muttered, With this affair.

He looked at me (or I suppose he did. I was looking at my feet) but he didn't say anything. Then finally he said, Let's move. And he started off down the street.

I trailed after him, feeling ineffectual and miserable.

Further up the street he stopped in front of the coffeehouse, opened the door and propelled me inside. The coffee is self-service and we helped ourselves and I followed Gabriel to a table over in a dark corner. The whole place is as dark as the inside of a pocket and was then deserted, which suited my state of mind. I didn't want to look at him (or anybody) and I didn't want anybody looking at me.

Gabriel started off coldly and abruptly. All right, he said. Let's have it. You don't get away with that we-can't-go-on-with-this stuff. This ain't no TV show. What's with you?

If I had not known before that he was angry, his using "ain't" would've told me. He uses words like that only when he's joking or when he's angry.

I tried to explain about the unseemliness (I think I even used that word) of anything between us because of his age, my age and my marriage.

He said he didn't buy any of that as the reason. He looked hard at me and said, Did you have a sudden rush of color to the head? Is that it?

For a minute I didn't get it. Then I did and I couldn't believe it. You must be kidding, I said. You've *got* to be.

He looked another long minute at me, then his face relaxed a little and he said, You wouldn't think like that, would you?

It was not a question but I answered it anyway and said I wouldn't think like that in a thousand years. I said it was everything *but* color. His youth, my age, my marriage, his life and my being a drag on him.

He took them up, ticking them off on his fingers as he went. The age difference had nothing to do with anything. We had never even noticed it. So why should we now?

My marriage (he said) was something he didn't know about since I didn't ever talk about it but it had to be that I wasn't all that attached to it or I wouldn't have come so close to him.

He stopped a minute. Then he went on and said, I don't believe that man you're married to really wants you, anyway. If he did he wouldn't leave you living like you do, practically a single woman.

He said the idea of my being a drag on him was a laugh. He said he had been happier in the time since he had known me than in all the time he had been in Cambridge; that he worked better, thought better, did everything better. How could I be a drag? What did I think I could do to him?

It was uncanny that while he was talking the record player had been giving out with "Mrs. Robinson." It was still giving out with "Mrs. Robinson."

And I said, Be a Mrs. Robinson, that's what.

He looked incredulous. Then he laughed. You hung up on the idea you're some character in a movie? he said, and he took my hand and clasped our fingers together and then he beat our combined fist up and down on the bench between us. Oh, Sophie, Sophie! he said and he shook his head.

I said it was not so crazy. I said there were a lot of similarities; that she was middle-aged and married and having this affair with a very young guy and she had tried to wreck the guy's life.

Boxes! he said. Categories! You never thought like this before. Why're you doing it now? You being Mrs. Robinson and us having an affair. You're Sophie, baby, and it's just you and me. You and me being together is what it's all about.

I sat there staring at the cup of coffee, thinking I should just get up and walk away from it. From him. From us. But everything he said sounded so right. And we *felt* so right together. It seemed as if it would be wrong to give it up. But, even as I thought that, another part of my mind was telling me to go.

The record was being replayed and I heard the words "Where have you gone, Joe DiMaggio?" and at the same time Gabriel turned my head around and said, Where have you gone, Sophie-darling-girl?

I'm here, I said. I was crazy. I wouldn't have left you.

We went to his room and, without a word, we went to bed. Afterwards, as we lay there, we talked the way people do who have narrowly escaped a terrible accident.

Later Gabriel walked with me to where I'd left the car and we got to laughing about something completely unimportant. We were practically falling into the street. Then, as the laughter let up, Gabriel said, Most people never have what we have in their entire lives.

He is always saying what I think and it must be that he really thinks it. I mean, there's no reason for him to think up things to please me. He could have dozens of girls, and I mean *girls,* not old ladies, and pretty and intelligent ones, and he wouldn't have to do a thing. To me he is the most beautiful man in the world but by anybody's standards he is an extraordinarily handsome man. He is tall (but not so tall he makes me feel like a dwarf), lean without being angular, and with a face that would be almost too perfect if it were not so strongly modeled. His forehead is very high and his hair starts back just where the forehead begins to curve. Then the hair rises like a crown in a modified Afro (he says he used to wish it were bushier but he supposed there had been too many whities in the woodpile). His eyes are remarkable . . . a warm, glowing brown as if they had a light behind them and they slant up, just a fraction, at the outside edges, giving him the look, in certain lights, of an ancient Mongol prince. Sometimes I think his eyes are his best feature but then I consider his nose which is strong and bony, almost hawklike, and I think it is perhaps the nose. But it is his mouth I like best. It is large but quite flat, (so much for "Negroid" mouths) and it turns up slightly just as his eyes do. His color depends so much on the light that it is hard to say just what it is. Sometimes it is almost as black as strong coffee, sometimes it gleams and makes me think of the color of the ocean when it is still and reflecting the blazing sun. Dear Gabriel, shall I compare you to a summer's day? And, summer being for me the best and happiest time, that is what I would do.

Admittedly, I am biased and look at him with the mote of affection in my eye but there is no question he is a very personable fellow and could find plenty of girls to do whatever he wanted to do, including screwing. So it cannot be that sex is all he wants from me. Indeed, considering my age (and how I wish I could stop considering it) and the fact that I was never a sex pot, it should surprise me that he wants that at all. It doesn't, however, surprise me and the reason it doesn't is contained in something he said this afternoon. We were lying in bed and he sort of laughed to himself. Then he said, Got a riddle for you. When is a screw more than a screw?

Obligingly, I asked when. And he said, When it is with somebody you feel you're already inside of.

How can I feel guilty about being with (forget that ugly word affair) a man like that? And I don't. Even with Ames, I didn't feel guilty about it. She and I were having dinner tonight in the kitchen and I tried to think of myself as a low, vicious thing, an adulterous, guilty mother. But I could not do it. I felt happy and maybe that feeling communicated itself to her because she seemed happier than usual herself and even seemed to enjoy (or at least not to mind) talking to me.

She was talking about school and the black studies class. And she said that it was hard for her to imagine the kind of people there must be out there who consider blacks different or inferior. I mean (she said), I know racists are for real. I see them on TV and I read about them. But I don't *know* any people like that. Color doesn't seem to count in Cambridge.

She is right about this little corner of the world we live in, color does not SEEM to count. Blacks and whites can go anywhere together and blacks can go most places and there is no outward reaction. But there is still plenty of feeling below the surface and not always very far below.

I was thinking about this during the evening as I was going around doing chores, putting clothes in the machines and ironing.

I thought of how shocked I had been by Gabriel's asking me if I had had a rush of color to the head. Considering it, I have to admit that it is not unreasonable to imagine that a middle-aged, middle-class, white woman would have strong reservations about being sexually involved with a black man. But it was only after much thought that I realized this.

I suddenly wondered why it is that I don't think, haven't thought, about having to conceal what Gabriel and I have. It hasn't entered my mind that anybody would ever think anything about seeing us together, in the streets, in a restaurant, in the movies, anywhere. And it dawns on me that the reason I haven't thought of it is because nobody *would* think there could be anything between a woman like me (to use Hibbard's phrase) a white, middle-aged, middle-class woman, and a young black man. People like me don't have affairs with people like Gabriel. (And they are right. As Gabriel said, this isn't an affair.) We are safe in a way that I would not be safe with a white man of whatever age. No matter how liberal and liberated the person might be, he would just not think, seeing me with Gabriel, that maybe we are sleeping together. He would think, There's Sophie with that black boy. She must be involved in some civil-rights thing or some other of her good works. And that's all there'd be to it.

I was ironing J.'s handkerchiefs when I happened to think of a conversation I had with Deb some time ago. We were talking about John and Kay, a couple who recently came here from New York. John is black and Kay is white and they were having trouble finding an apartment. Kay would see an apartment and everything would be fine. Then she'd bring John to look at it and suddenly the owner would discover some repairs that had to be made, or somebody's mother needed it, or a mistake had been made in placing it on the market in the first place. (Oh yes, Ames, color *does* count in Cambridge.)

Anyway, Deb and I were trying to find them a place. And it was Deb who actually did get them one. And she liked them. I know she liked them. But that day, she said to me, You know, Sophie, it is the most awful thing but I positively cringe when I imagine Kay in bed with John.

And tonight, when I remembered her saying that, it struck me so that I stood there staring mindlessly at the ironing board until the smell of the scorched handkerchief brought me back.

I was, I remember, not shocked by her statement but astounded. What I wondered was why was she imagining them, or anybody, in bed?

She, in turn, seemed astounded that I did not. She said that most people do (imagine people in bed) and that I must be very repressed if I didn't.

Afterwards, I set myself to imagining people having interc. I tried Deb and Marsden, and then Kay and John. But, although I got both couples undressed and each on a bed, I could not get them to do anything; they lay there inert and lifeless. I decided that Deb was right, that I am repressed in the worst way and later I told Ass Bird about this. He asked *why* I wanted to fantasy couples having interc. I told him that apparently everybody else did and it seemed as if I should at least be *able* to. He then suggested that I was trying to compete with Deb!

Anyway, tonight standing there burning up the handkerchiefs, I suddenly saw Gabriel's face and then I saw us in bed and the desire for him was so great that I had to hold onto the ironing board to keep from dissolving onto the floor.

It does seem that I *can* imagine interc. And it also seems clear that I do not cringe from a black man, at least if the man is Gabriel.

But then I thought of something else Deb said, in that same conversation. She said that it was wonderful that the kids didn't have these feelings (of difference, of strangeness) about blacks and that eventually they would integrate. But for *us* (she said) the old ways of thinking and behaving are just too ingrained. No matter how much we might want to, we can never get rid of them.

I argued that some people did. Kay, for just one example. Deb agreed that there were exceptions but they were very rare. And she wondered if *they* didn't have their moments of doubt and even repugnance.

I said that I didn't know about her but I certainly had my moments of doubt and repugnance about the fine white man I am married to.

She laughed; called me "an incurable romantic" and said she hoped my "idealism" would never be put to the test.

So here I am asking myself if I "picked" Gabriel in order to put myself to the test. But I *didn't* pick Gabriel. He was just there; he spoke to me first and since he is sort of in charge at the Center, it was he I had the most to do with. And I liked him. I would've liked him just as much if he'd been white. Only he's black so I like it that he's black. Because it is one of his attributes. Not because I need to demonstrate something or other about blacks.

I suppose there are all kinds of reasons why I don't have any reservations about Gabriel's color: reasons such as early training (my parents' lack of bias), childhood religious training (Quakers believe that *every* person is a child of God . . . and insofar as I believe there is a god, I still believe that) and never forgetting my affection for Bertie.

But maybe the simplest explanation is that once upon a time when I was lying in my cradle a fairy godmother said, One day you will meet a handsome Black Knight and you will cherish him all the days of your life. And I have and I'm afraid I will.

Tuesday, Dec. 2

To the Center briefly. Only long enough to see Gabriel, say hello and be glad he is there, that he *is*.

A day of duties and errands: to have my teeth cleaned, to buy shorts and shirts for J., to shop for groceries, to see Mrs. K. who is down with flu and to take her some food; home to do all the things Mrs. K. won't be doing this week. Change the beds, clean the bathrooms, scrub the kitchen floor, etc.

Ames at Gretchie's for dinner so I had a sandwich and read the paper, becoming apoplectic over the talk of impeaching Justice Douglas. It is so obviously just a retaliation for the defeat of Haynsworth that I can't believe they will get away with it. But that's pretty stupid of me . . . "they" seem to get away with just about anything. The only time this country has looked good to me lately is when I read Solzhenitsyn (what a great man as well as writer he is). At least we do not have political repression to that extent, yet.

Cissy called and was more cheerful. Said Little Soph (who has been home some time now) has eschewed her drug pals and is taking a course in carpentry. Cissy doesn't know why carpentry but said she was not looking any gift horse in the mouth.

I am feeling very uncomfortable about J.'s return tomorrow. He left an unhappy but faithful wife. He will come back to a happy (despite everything, I *am*) but faithless one. I would feel sure he could read the Scarlet

Letter on my forehead except that he has never read any of the other messages written there.

I know now I am not going to tell him. I thought at first that I should. But now it seems to me it would be a cruel, senseless thing to do.

Once he knew, he would not (I think) be able to stay under the same roof with me and it seems wicked to force him out. Not only because it would deprive him of his home and children but because it would deprive *them* of him. And there is no question of my going. I am not going to leave my children. However much they seem to want to flee their home and parents, we still have to be here if only to give them something to flee from.

But it is one thing to sit here and write about what I am going to do. It is another thing to actually live with this deception. And I get that falling-elevator feeling in my stomach even as I think about it.

I wish I had somebody to talk to. But there is nobody I can talk to about this. Of course I will tell Ass Bird. There would be no sense in continuing with him if I did not. But I don't expect much help from him. He will very likely find it hard to believe that a woman in my position (whatever that is) could have a sexual relationship with a man who I am sure will seem to Ass Bird quite outside the pale (whatever *that* is). I have often thought Ass Bird is pretty uptight about a lot of things and might profit by having his own head shrunk. Or maybe his trouble is that it has been shrunk too much.

Wednesday, Dec. 3

I am writing this late at night in the guest room where I am now living.

This morning Ames told me, quite casually, that she is moving in with the Steins for a while.

I had just come back from marketing and I was standing with my back to her at the counter unpacking the bags. Her words stopped me dead. They seemed to go right through the middle of my chest. I could feel the small round hole they made. I was holding a plastic-wrapped chicken and I clutched it to that opening between my ribs and I croaked, Oh?

Then I got my voice going better and I said, I know the service isn't great around here but I thought the accommodations were pretty comfortable.

Oh, *Mother!* she said in that do-drop-dead tone. I'm *serious*.

I still didn't move, just clutched the chicken and kept my eyes on the tree outside the window. I'm serious, too, I said. When you lose your star boarder, you naturally want to know what's wrong and if it's something you can fix.

She said it was nothing that could be fixed. It's just (she said) that I have to free myself from your domination, yours and Dad's.

Our *what?* I said, remarking somewhere in my head that I was probably going into a catatonic state because I could not seem to move at all, not even to put the chicken down.

I don't suppose you mean to do it, she said. But you treat me as if I were a child, always prying and bossing and . . . well, I talked it over with Gretchie and Mrs. Stein and we agreed it would be the best thing for all concerned.

Amazed that my voice was so steady, I said that I was sorry to know that living with us was so difficult.

She said it wasn't so difficult; just crippling.

I asked why it was crippling and she said it would be hopeless to try to explain because we are so full of middle-class values that we could never understand.

I didn't say anything, just hung onto the chicken and stared out the window. I had some kind of idea that if I didn't move maybe all this would disappear; that maybe it would never have happened.

She came over and standing there at the end of the counter she looked at me and said, Why do you keep holding that chicken? There's a leak in that bag and you've got chicken gunk all down the front of you.

When do you think you'll come back? I asked.

She said she hadn't thought. Maybe a few weeks or months. Then, sharply she said, Mother! For pete's sake, put down that chicken!

I looked down at the bird, surprised he was still there, and I said it was hard to give up what had become a bosom companion.

She laughed and said, Oh, you're all right!

There was enormous relief in her voice and it was still there as she went on to say she was glad I was not taking this personally; that actually she thought we were pretty good as parents but it was a question of life styles.

That relief made me realize I had to help her and I got my feet unglued and went to the fridge. Putting the poor, leaking bird in (knowing I'd have to clean up after it later), I said briskly that I hoped she wouldn't mind if I called Gwen Stein, just to sort of show an interest. She said she wouldn't mind at all. Then I asked if she'd wait around until her father came back; that I was going to get him soon. And she said very agreeably that she'd be glad to.

Then I went calmly out of the kitchen, hurried upstairs to the bathroom where the tears spurted out of my eyes like a fountain of hot acid. I put my face against J.'s robe which was hanging on the door and when I finally moved away I was almost surprised the tears had not burned holes in it, they had been so hot on my cheeks.

By the time I had washed my face and changed my dress I was under control enough to call Gwen Stein. I meant to sound casual and I think I did but it was nothing compared to her casualness which was monumental. Still, I suppose her attitude is understandable when you consider that Gretchie is the last of 6 assorted children; she and Wayne each having had 2 kids by former marriages and then 2 more to cement, if that is the right word, their own union.

I unpacked the groceries, cleaned up the mess the poor old bird had made in the fridge, rewrapped him and put him in the freezer, wondering if I'll ever be able to cook and eat him (talk about sloppy sentimentality! Still, the old thing does seem like a friend).

I heard Ames singing upstairs in her room and I know I should've been happy that *she* was happy but I wasn't. It made that hole in my chest start aching all over again. But I gave myself a stern talking-to; reminding myself that I had accepted what had to be accepted (after all, we cannot lock her up) and with pretty good grace and that she *would* be back and that I had to present it to J. in that light. And then it was time to go to the airport to get him.

The plane was on time for once and as J. drove us home I asked him in my usual pro forma way about the meetings. They had been discouraging. He says the underdeveloped countries run harder and harder but fall further behind. And he did sound discouraged as he said they are not just relatively but absolutely worse off.

I hated to discourage him further by telling him about Ames but I did. He hit the ceiling or would have if his seat belt hadn't been fastened. Then he quieted down and wanted to know what is the matter with us. I said I didn't think there was anything the matter with us (which is of course not true but I meant in re Ames and there I do think we've been as OK as parents can ever be); that it is her age and the times, both of which are revolutionary. He objected to that word (our own glorious revolution always seems to slip his mind) but characteristically practical, he said there is nothing we can do but accept it so we might as well do it with good grace.

And that is what we did. He tried to chat a little with Ames but she wasn't giving either of us the time of day and finally he said, Well, keep in touch. And she said she would and she left.

J. went to the Univ. to collect his mail. I started a wash and as I was sorting light and dark I came on Ames's blue jeans and I held them up and looked at them. They had the imprint of her body and I could see her standing there in them, and then suddenly she and the jeans shrank and I saw her at age 3 or 4 in one of her first pairs of jeans . . . cute and round and laughing (she used to laugh so much) . . . and I thought my heart would crack in two as I realized she is really gone forever.

Oh, I know she'll come back, physically, but she is gone from me for good. Don't tell me it has to be so. I know it. But that does not make it less painful. I saw her being born . . . and I remembered how proud I was of us both (although, of course, I did not know it was Ames in there struggling to get out) that we were accomplishing this birth so neatly and, for me, so happily. And I remembered how I had raised myself on my elbows when Dr. Barnes said, She's here!

She was all white powdery-looking and her face scrunched up as she cried and she was beautiful. I suppose I will never in this world be as happy as I was then. Now she has gone and this is the real pain . . . the real delivery.

When J. returned I made him a sandwich and as he ate, I made some comment about Ames's leaving and then I said, Going to be kind of empty around here without her, isn't it?

Not especially, he said pouring himself a beer. She wasn't here much anyway.

No, I said, but she hadn't really left us. Not the permanent, irrevocable way she has left us now.

Why don't you stop thinking of yourself? he said, tossing the beer can in the trash as if he wished it were me. Why don't you think of how good it is for *her* to grow up and away?

Whenever I express any feeling (I said) you always say I am thinking of myself as if I were a selfish monster, as if it were abnormal to have feelings of loss and regret and longing. (I said this quite reasonably, I thought.)

Your feelings *are* abnormal, he said. You're always

feeling loss about things you can't, in the nature of things, keep and you always regret things you can't help. It doesn't seem to me that psychiatrist has done you much good.

No, I said coldly. No more than you. You are both as thick-skinned as alligators and about as perceptive.

Thank you very much, he said stiffly.

And thank you for nothing, I said as I flung the clothes in the dryer. I come to you for comfort and you give me a stone.

I could say the same about you. (He said this sort of backed up against the sink and it crossed my mind that he looked kind of forlorn, but I was too mad to let it do more than cross and go right out again.)

Then why don't you say it? I yelled at him as I banged the dryer door. Why don't you ever *say* what you feel? I am sick to death of your goddamn stiff upper lip.

And I stomped out of the kitchen and went upstairs. I had already planned to sleep in the guest room and I had made up the bed, so I took my small pillow from the Giant Bed (I always think of it in the Italian, the Letto Matrimoniale) and my books from the table.

Later I was in bed reading when he stuck his head in the door and asked if I would not please come to bed in our room.

I said I couldn't. Then he said he sometimes thought I provoked quarrels with him so I would have an excuse not to sleep with him.

I said I had not done that this time. And it is true that I didn't but it's also true that it gave me an excuse to do what I was going to do anyway. Or not do.

I was reading Leonard Woolf's "Downhill All the Way" (a wonderful title . . . it is the last, so far, vol. of his autobiog.) and usually it grabs me but my mind kept falling away from it as I wondered why it is that I do not feel I should tell J. about Gabriel. And why I do not even feel guilty about it. I have never deliberately concealed anything important from him. Or even unimportant things, if they seemed important to me. But about this I feel no compulsion to tell him.

Maybe it is because it seems that he has, in a way, abandoned me. Oh, he wants me as a wife, I guess, but he does not want ME, the "hyper-emotional, over-reactive, too-violent" (all his words) me. It is almost as if he had given me a license to take that person elsewhere.

I am two people with two lives: the one who lives here and is real only with and in relation to the children and the other one who lives with Gabriel and is real all the time. And the one life has no connection with the other. Except that I cannot have interc. with J. and sleep with Gabriel and I am not going to stop sleeping with Gabriel. And I am not going to think about it either.

Friday, Dec. 5

Quick lunch with Deb today. We long ago made our amends to each other for Thanksgiving. She saying I am her best and oldest friend and me saying I will always care about her no matter what either of us does or says (which is true).

She has started going to those "Over Thirty" dinners at the Unitarian (I think) church but she is depressed because Mr. Right has not appeared after only two dinners. I urged her to keep on and told her to forget about finding a soul mate (pretty funny remark coming from me, that is), just to find some man she can do things with, like sailing for one. She used to love to sail. She said all that reminded her too much of the happy days with Marsden.

She told me, by the way, that I am looking wonderful and wanted to know if I am using something new. I said it was very new and when she pressed me I said it was early to bed, early to rise.

Deb walked me to the Center where I continued trying to write up what we know so far about the workings of the Draft Lottery. About four Gabriel came for me and we went home and to bed and we lay there and talked and then we fell asleep and awoke late and I had to hurry home to fix dinner. It is really odd how this double life does not seem to bother me (I say "seem" because maybe it does and I don't know it).

Yesterday Ass Bird said I seem happier lately and then he said, I told you the pills would take effect.

I said I hadn't taken the pills for weeks. He was annoyed and said I shouldn't have stopped without asking him. Then he asked what did I think had been helping me.

Maybe he thought I would say His Therapy but I said I had at last done what I'd said I should do . . . get myself a lover.

He sat up straighter and asked who he is.

I said, He is a sweet, intelligent, loving young man about half my age—well, he's twenty-five anyhow. Then I told AB how I had met Gabriel at the Center (I had mentioned him before but just in passing) and about the awful Thanksgiving dinner. And then (I said) he kissed me and that put me under a spell so I ran off with him and we went to an enchanted field and there we slept with each other. And he is beautiful. Black and beautiful.

Have you given him a name? AB asked.

His name is Gabriel, I said, but of course he's really my Black Knight.

By now AB had slumped back and was running his finger around in his ear (always a sign he is bored), and he said to continue with the fantasy.

I laughed and said I knew it sounded like a dream but it was very real.

He said he knew I had an odd sense of humor but I must not insist on his taking my fantasies for the truth.

I started to protest again that it was not a fantasy. And then it occurred to me that AB had a point, not the one he thought he had, but a point all the same, and I said, You know, it *is* as if I had invented him. He is my heart's desire. Everything about him pleases me. He is exactly what I would have chosen had I been choosing.

But you did choose him, AB said.

Not exactly, I said (thinking that at last he believed me and we were talking about reality). It was really Gabriel who chose me. I mean, at the beginning, when I went to the Counseling Center that first day, it was *Gabriel* who spoke to *me* and it was Gabriel who persuaded me to stay. And then it became a friendship, the kind of friendship that's rare at any age, the kind one almost never begins at my age. Sometimes I used to think it was a dream, that I couldn't be having this happy, easy friendship with this young man, that he couldn't accept me as an equal.

That is, of course, why you made him black, AB said.

Come again? I said, not understanding.

You made him black and you did so because only that way could you feel that you were his equal. Of course (he went on in his heavy, flat voice), there were other reasons why you made him black. The desire of white women, especially intellectual types, to have a primitive black-skinned lover is very common. So it is perfectly understandable, on many levels, that you fantasied a black man.

I stared at him. Then I said, One of us is crazy, man.

He smiled a tiny, private smile and said that he was now habituated to my pattern of humor and that he supposed by now he knew how to take it.

After all (he said), you could hardly expect me to believe that a woman in your position, a woman with great sexual repressions, a woman who has never even kissed another man since her marriage, that such a woman would casually commit adultery! Then he gave that tiny smile again and he said, As you yourself said this boy is your heart's desire.

But he's real! I said.

Oh, I don't doubt there is such a boy at this Center. But you did not have sex with him. This is very similar to an earlier fantasy of yours, the one where you imagined yourself going off to the South Pole with some explorer.

But it's not at all the same thing! I said in an agony of frustration. That was Ernest Shackleton I imagined going off with. Ernest Shackleton who was a real polar explorer and who died before I was born. I mean, of course I wasn't going off to the South Pole and certainly not with a dead man.

And this is a black boy (AB said it as if I had just proved his point). Almost half your age, as you said. And, suddenly, after years of being a prisoner of your superego to the extent that you can hardly have relations with your husband, you throw off all your self-imposed restrictions and have sex with this wholly unsuitable young black . . . and in a field!

What the hell's wrong with a field? I said (I was both angry *and* frustrated by now).

If it had been a real assignation, AB said, you would have gone to a motel or to this boy's room. I believe you said he has one. There is some reason why you picked this field. It has some importance in your subconscious.

It *is* important, I said. And it's quite conscious. It's because I saw a movie, some time ago in my days of loneliness, and it was about a couple who wandered hand in hand all night in a field. There was something about it that really struck me so when it turned out that Gabriel and I were actually in a field, it made me think of how that yearning to be with somebody, to be close to somebody, had been realized. But it was a real movie and a real field, don't you see?

I see (AB said with a satisfied air) that you put yourself where you yearned to be. Then he reared back in his chair (and I wished he'd fall over backwards) and he said, I find this a very satisfactory development. Your repressions are beginning to surface and once you have worked through this fantasy I think we may begin to see an improvement in your relations with your husband.

I looked at him for a long time but I could see nothing on his face except bland satisfaction. And for just an instant my heart almost stopped as it occurred to me that I might be insane. Could I possibly have imagined going off with Gabriel and sleeping with him in that field? But then I remembered that I had taken a piece of the grass, or whatever the stubble was, from the field and stuck it in my pocket. And that I had it at home (it is right here now). I knew I had been in that field and if I had been there I had been there with Gabriel and if I had been there with Gabriel I had slept with him.

It sounds insane now as I write this that I had to go through all that in my mind. But, for a minute or two, AB had me thinking I might actually be crazy.

And I said to him, Did you ever see a movie called "Gaslight"?

He said no and was it the one with the field in it.

I said no; that it was about a husband who tried to drive his wife crazy by making certain things happen to her and afterwards fixing it so that it looked as if those things could not possibly have happened.

He asked if I thought my husband was doing this.

And I saw it was hopeless and I just shook my head.

He waited awhile but I didn't say anything, being struck numb and dumb by the realization that here was a therapist who could drive his patients to the loony bin by convincing them that what they think is reality and what is, in fact, reality is a product of their disturbed minds. And I began to wonder how many of his patients were now wandering around McLean or some other retreat for those who cannot distinguish between fact and fancy.

AB then asked if I was having any sex.

Only with Shackleton, I said.

Then there was a long silence which AB broke by asking me if I was masturbating. I didn't bother to remind him that I don't masturbate. I just said, Not right this minute.

Finally, AB said to have J. call him for an appointment; said it was time to give J. an evaluation of me.

I asked if he was going to tell J. to commit me.

AB said, That is not indicated.

I wonder, if I really put my mind to it, whether I could convince AB that Gabriel is real. But why bother? If the man so blindly misinterprets everything that is said to him, he could not help me with the truth even if he were brought to see that it is the truth.

When I think of all the things I have been thinking about, all the things I would have liked to tell him! I used to worry that I was undersexed and then, lately, with J. the worry has come back because I didn't want to have interc. with him. But now, since Gabriel, I know, once and for all, that I am normal sexually. It is only that I do not have what some people seem to have: a free-floating sexual urge. My desire is there all right, but it only manifests itself when there is somebody around with whom I want to screw. And I wanted to tell this to AB because it seemed important but of course there is no sense in talking about what I have learned from Gabriel when, according to AB, there is no Gabriel.

The more I think about that incredible session with AB, the more it seems to me that this so-called therapy has a built-in Catch 22. If I am sane enough to see that AB is wrong about what is reality, then I am, by definition, insane because it is AB who decides what is reality. If I believe AB's definition of reality, then I am, in fact, insane because AB is, in fact, wrong.

I know I don't have many marbles (and fewer than when I started with him) but I have just enough to know that if I stayed with this character any longer I should deserve anything I might get, including a prefrontal lobotomy.

Saturday, Dec. 6

Up early this a.m. and had done some laundry, cleaned up the downstairs, read the paper and done the Xword by the time J. came down a little before nine.

As he drank his coffee and devoured the front page he asked me what I was going to do today.

He was arrayed in his Going-to-Meeting clothes (as opposed to his Just-Going-to-the-Univ. or Working-at-Home clothes) so I knew that whatever I was doing it would not be something with him.

I said I would probably go to the Center.

He said he was glad I had found something to do that interested me and I heard in his voice that same tone of relief that used to be in mine when the children would announce some project that would keep them busy and out of my hair.

And I wondered (as I have increasingly lately) if there is something inherently wrong with marriage as an institution and not just with J. and me as inmates of that Institution. And that gave rise to thoughts on Women's Lib., which I won't go into now except to say that wifehood is the only (legal) occupation that I know of where the employee is expected to have sexual relations with the employer and where, indeed, this obligation to screw has been elevated to a moral and psychological imperative.

After ingesting the front page and the editorials, J. took off, reminding me of the Beckwiths' dinner tonight. Then I went to the Center where Gabriel already was and it was like having the sun turned on to walk in and see him look up and smile. He has a smile I cannot describe. It is, in one word, warmth.

We closed up the office at noon. To the room and had lunch. He had a letter from his mother in Birmingham which he read to me. She is a nurse and works in a well-baby clinic (which is technically integrated but in fact is not because it is in a Negro neighborhood). She writes nice letters, realistically pessimistic but funny and cheerful withal.

I asked Gabriel if he had a picture of her but he doesn't so I asked him to describe her.

I can do better than that, he said. You want to see my Mam, you put on your coat and I'll take and show you the spittin' image of her.

I asked where we were going but he wouldn't say; just took my arm and led me along the street. Pretty soon I could see we were nearing the Fogg and the Busch-Reisinger. She's in a Museum? I asked.

He said yes and in a few minutes we turned into the Fogg. He turned us left and down the hall through the Chinese rooms and then he stopped before a painting. It was labeled "Head of a Bodhisattva" and it was of a beautiful person who looked female (but I later learned is not) with brown skin, green eyebrows, very pink lips, and a wonderfully serene look.

My Mam's eyebrows aren't green, Gabriel said. She doesn't have a crown-thing on her head and her lips aren't so red but, that to one side, she is my Mam.

He said he'd discovered her when he first came to Boston and now he looked in every now and again just to say hello. Those Buddhists, he said, are pretty good cats. My Mam would fit right in with them. She believes, like they do, that all life is shit.

I said then she must've been at odds with his father (because I know Gabriel's father didn't believe anything was shit, maybe not even shit).

They never had words about it, Gabriel said. She believed what she believed and he believed what he believed. I think she was sorry for him, though. Daddy thought life should be happy so he suffered all the time because it isn't. Mam thinks suffering is the natural order so to her anything good is a gift and she says Thanks and enjoys.

I wondered aloud which he was more like, his mother or his father.

They both left their imprint on me, he said. Then he grinned and said, But when I got my head screwed on right I take after my Mam. And you, Sophie-baby, could sure take a leaf from them Buddhists. And my Mam. You got to learn to rise above the shit, baby, rise above it.

To what? I asked. To where?

To whatever you believe in. You the philosopher in this family, he said. You must've already decided where you're standing and why.

I told him I used to know where I stood but I didn't know for sure anymore about anything. Take Aristotle, I said. I used to believe in his definition of happiness, that it's the activity of the rational part of the soul in accordance with reason throughout a whole life. But now (I said) I do not think this is true for most people and I doubt it could ever be true for most people and if it is not true for most people then this cannot be a world in which rational activity can bring happiness.

He had his arm around my shoulders and now he

squeezed them and said, Let's start on back. Which we did and as we walked he said most people are not rational and never would be but that didn't mean reason couldn't be my bag. But first I had to see what's given and accept it.

I took immediate umbrage at that and started off saying that was the worst kind of religiously inspired claptrap.

He interrupted to tell me to shut my big mouth and to open my little head for just one minute; that he didn't mean accept as good or as unalterable but accept as a fact whatever is. You are all the time (he said) getting your bowels in an uproar over What Is. You can change some things and some things you can't, but you got to accept the *fact* of whatever is.

Then he spoke of going back south to teach. It is something I want to do (he said) something I can do, something I know I'll be pretty good at because I accept the shitty system as a fact. I want to change it, sure, and I plan to do what I can but I don't waste my time thinking how awful it is that the shit hit the fan when I was born.

All the way back to the room we went on talking, about his teaching, about the system, about Aristotle, the Buddhists, about Hobbes, and about him and about me and then we were back at the room and we went to bed and I realized that this at least is one thing I accept as What Is. It is an astonishing, continuing happiness and I take it as a gift and I do enjoy.

About 6:30 I tore myself away and even then I was late and J. was annoyed that I was.

By the time you get dressed, he said, and we get there, they'll have finished dinner.

I hurried up to dress, thinking that if we arrived two hours late we would still not be late for dinner.

And I was, I am sorry to say, right. Everybody was drinking when we got there and an hour later everybody was still drinking and it was not until after 9:30 that the dining room door was opened and what I felt would be my ultima cena was unveiled. It was a large and sumptuous buffet but as I looked at us all doing the ritual shuffle, making the ritual remarks . . . some of us staggering from hunger, some from too much to drink . . . I thought that large buffet dinners are certainly high on my list of civilization's discontents. In my next life I will never go to any dinner party of more than six people.

One good thing about the evening: I met an Indian (an Indian Indian), a lovely man, and we talked during and after dinner about Buddhism. He didn't drink either which is what made us pals to start with, trying as we were to fight off the wine and get a drop of water. He had a beautiful smile and was wonderfully funny and I was very sorry to know that he was only visiting and was, in fact, leaving the next day. He invited me (us, of course) to visit him and gave me his address in Bombay (which I may not be able to use in this life but certainly will in my next). He has three grown sons and a wife who is a doctor whom he said I would like and vice versa. I asked what his wife is like and he said, Like you, she defies description.

I knew that must be a compliment (because he clearly did like me) so I said I would take it as such. He said it was the highest of compliments and I felt as if a garland had been placed on my head.

Going home, J. said, You and Rama (the Indian) certainly had your heads together. I must say you made it hard for other people to talk to him.

That so took me aback that I could only open my mouth like a fish gasping for air.

He was the guest of honor, J. said. Or didn't you know that?

I said I didn't but if I had I don't suppose I would've behaved any differently. Mr. Rama is a grown man, I said, and he could have got away if he wanted to.

Why would he want to? J. said. With you hanging on his every word and laughing every two seconds. He's got a reputation as a great lady-charmer and after seeing you I suppose it is deserved.

I said coldly that I supposed it was.

There was a silence and then J. said with considerable force (almost anger), Why don't you ever circulate?

I asked him if he had any idea how ridiculous he sounded. There was another silence and then he said, I just find it hard to understand why your depression seems to disappear with everybody except me.

There was a lot I could've said to that and a lot I would've said a few weeks ago. But now, with Gabriel sitting there between us, there was nothing to say.

When we got home and were in the living room turning off the lights, J. tried to put his arm around me and he said, Isn't there any way we can mend things?

I bolted away from him and said, No, not now.

He started out of the room, then he stopped and asked how long I thought we could continue to live like this.

And I said that was up to him.

He didn't say anything, just went on up. I turned on the TV and watched one of those fantastically bad movies and tried not to think of J.'s question nor of any of the other questions that life with Gabriel raises.

After a while I was able to turn off the movie and the questions and come up here with the thought of Gabriel clutched to my bosom like a precious mustard seed.

Tuesday, Dec. 9

Yesterday Gabriel assembled a whole ream of his typed stuff and asked me to go through it with a cold, fine-tooth comb. Which I did but there was nothing to comb. When he came back from school I told him it was a great piece of scholarship and a fascinating story. Don't change a word, I said. Submit it like it is and you're in like Flynn.

He was pleased but said I must not think he is finished. There is, he said, more to do. The last days before the great reversals and the return of White Supremacy.

I said he should call it the First Great Reversal as we are now well into the Second. And I got going on the Chicago Black Panther Shootings (the whole thing looks like a dirty Government Plot but I will not go into it here as I am trying to practice keeping my cool . . . if I can ever find it).

I was even then beginning to rave a little when Gabriel said, Easy, girl, easy. If you let it get to you like this, why, they have done one of the things they set out to do. You got to keep your cool and look down on them.

But you also have to *do* something, I said.

He had been making coffee and he handed me a cup and sat down on the bed beside me. Worrying isn't doing one damn thing, he said. Then he smoothed my hair back off my forehead and he said, Relax and let your mind sit awhile on some of the good things.

I asked him to tell me 2 good things I could sit my mind on.

Haynsworth, he said. Haynsworth kept off the Supreme Court. Now that is something. And that Italian you were telling me about the other day, what was his name? He said he'd give part of his Nobel money to work against the War.

I said that was Salva Luria and there were not many Salvas and that undoubtedly someone even worse than Haynsworth would be appointed to the Court and anyway two swallows do not a summer make.

He said I was a regular Jeremiah. What ever gave you the idea, he asked, that you got a right to even *two* swallows? And you telling me you majored in Philosophy! Only the other day you were talking about Hobbes and what he said about life, that it's nasty, brutish and short. That's not just something out of some book. That's like it *is*. Come on, girl, get with it and give thanks you're alive.

I said he sounded like Norman Vincent Peale or Oral Roberts and how could I give thanks that I was alive when . . .

But he cut me off by saying, Shut your mouth. Then he pushed me back on the bed and said, And let *me* give thanks that you're alive.

And in no time I was glad that we were both alive. Afterwards, while he was in the shower and I was remaking the bed, I got to thinking how like and how very unlike this argument was to many I have had with J. Some of the words are even the same but the feeling is totally different. I never feel with J. that we are both trying to reach the same end: an understanding of what it's all about. And with J. I almost never end by thinking that I am wrong or that my point of view is lopsided. Also with J. our arguments never end happily and never in bed.

We went to the Center but for once there were so many people working that we left. Got sandwiches at Elsie's and ate them sitting on a bench looking at the chilly Charles. Before Gabriel is through with me I shall be ready to join a Polar Expedition. He likes to be out in any weather at all and he would cheerfully picnic on an ice floe or even, I do believe, sleep with me on one.

We got to talking again about family. Gabriel seems fascinated by mine, says he thinks they must've been really far out which makes me laugh when I think of my eminently respectable parents.

Still, I suppose they were far out in a way. Certainly they were not like most parents. They would never, never tell us what to do: Mother relying on that still, small voice to tell us what we *ought* to do and Father relying on our instincts to tell us what we *wanted* to do. Gabriel says my trouble is that I have always thought I should want to do what I ought to do and have not realized that sometimes I ought to do what I want to do. (All-Wise Dr. D. used to say something like that.)

We stopped in briefly at the Fogg to check on Gabriel's Mam. Then he had a seminar.

I drove out to Concord to buy another skirt like the green corduroy that Gabriel likes. I wear it with a pink sweater (of which I too am fond) and one day when he was smoothing the skirt and the sweater I asked him how come he had such a thing about them.

He considered a moment and then he said, Because they are watermelon colors and all niggers love watermelon.

Whether it was what he said or the way he said it (he would've been a great comic actor, he has such a dry, deadpan manner sometimes), I laughed until I almost cried.

We seem to laugh so much. I don't put it all down here because there is so much I'd never have time to do anything else. Like today, sitting there by the Charles. I didn't write about that but I will now because it is a part of our good times and I ought to write more about those and less about the gloomy things (putting my mind on good things as instructed).

Anyway, we were sitting there talking when an elderly lady (I mean *really* elderly) came by with a little dog on a leash. He was frisky and straining at the leash and finally he got right away from her and dashed off down to the water's edge.

She called him, Hartley, Hartley (or maybe it was Heartly?) and she took some tentative steps but it was clear she was not up to chasing him.

So Gabriel took off and in a few minutes he came back with Hartley in tow.

I had been standing beside her and as he neared us she said to me, Oh, isn't he the nicest man? I do think he's just the *nicest* man.

Then she thanked Gabriel and scolded Hartley and thanked Gabriel again and as she started off she said to us, I love you young people. I think you're just *cunning*.

And of course that made us laugh.

The dog being named Hartley reminded Gabriel of a joke which Rosenblum (his adviser and the source of a lot of his jokes) told him and he told it to me as we were walking back.

It seems there was a Jew in a railway carriage in Poland and also in this carriage was a Polish army officer. The officer had a dog to whom he kept feeding bits of food.

Sit, Yankel (the officer would say). Or beg, Yankel.

And the Jew watched this and shook his head over and over.

What's the matter with you, Jew? the officer said. Why do you keep shaking your head?

Poor dog, said the Jew, shaking his head.

Why "poor dog"? the officer said indignantly. What's wrong with my dog?

Poor dog, the Jew said again. If his name weren't Yankel he could be an officer in the Polish Army.

End of joke.

Now Gabriel thought that was very funny. He even laughed out loud as he told it. I didn't crack a smile; in fact, I grimaced.

Gabriel said, You didn't think it was funny?

I said I did not.

He said, Maybe you didn't get it then. And he started to explain it.

I got it all right, I said. I just don't like it, that's all.

But why not? he wanted to know.

I think it's a mean, cruel joke, I said.

But it's a Jewish joke, Gabriel said. It's *told* by Jews.

I said I wouldn't care if it was told by Jesus Christ himself, I still wouldn't like it. Then I said, Listen, suppose that joke were about a black man and the Grand Dragon of the Ku Klux Klan and they are riding in a train and the Grand Dragon has this dog named Rastus and the Black Man shakes his head and all and finally he says,

Poor dog. If his name weren't Rastus he could be a Grand Dragon in the Ku Klux Klan. Would you think that was funny?

And I looked at him and he was *laughing*.

Oh, well, I said. I give up. And I laughed too.

And it dawns on me (or re-dawns on me for surely I must've known this before) that Aristotle's happiness involves a right functioning of the whole person and that this is what I have (and do) with Gabriel. There is joy, pleasure and delight in simply Being. And this is what I have not felt in so long that I have almost forgotten what it is like to forget oneself and to experience being alive as What Is.

Friday, Dec. 12

For the last few weeks, starting back before Thanksgiving, a crazy thing has been going on at the Center between Gabriel and one Fernstermaker. I say "crazy" because Gabriel's behavior has been so atypical and today when it surfaced like some sinister submarine it turned out to be even crazier than I had thought.

One Fernstermaker is a very young (not yet draftable), very Southern (white) freshman with bad eyes who came to the Center asking would his eyes get him a deferment. After much back and forth it developed that nobody could translate the Govt.'s regulations into layman's language so Fernstermaker set himself to do this. He got hold of some sympathetic eye doctor and he wrote it all down so you can have some idea of where your eyes are at and now it is in a portfolio which we call Fernstermaker's Eyes.

While he was working on this Fernstermaker hung around the Center and he has continued to hang around, not actually counseling but running errands, making phone calls and helping in lots of ways.

Now most people like Fernstermaker. *I* do very much. I am charmed by his kinky blond hair, his myopic blue eyes, his ratty old metal-rimmed specs and his small, slightly protruding teeth which make him look like George, the lovable hamster David used to have.

But Gabriel took an immediate dislike to Fernstermaker and has acted as if F. were the fingernail down his blackboard. This has made for considerable unpleasantness (at least it has seemed considerable to me) because Fernstermaker idolizes Gabriel. He seems dimly aware that Gabriel does not warm to him but he keeps right on trying. The poor boy will leap to his feet, which are enormous, whenever Gabriel enters the room and he will produce a chair and say, Right heah, Gabe, heah's a cheer. Or, Yew wanta cuppa cawfee, Gabe? Yew sit right theah, Ah'll bring it to you.

Gabriel will turn his back on the cheer, he will curl his lip at the cawfee and, in general, he is hateful to Fernstermaker. This has puzzled me because I have never seen Gabriel be unkind to anyone before. I have told him that he is rough on Fernstermaker and I have asked him why. Back in the beginning he said it was because Fernstermaker was an "itch" (whatever the hell that means) but he would try to be better to him. But he has not tried and lately he has been worse than ever.

Today he was particularly churlish and afterwards

when we were walking to his room, I said to him, You are a bastard and you ought to be ashamed of the crummy way you treat Fernstermaker.

Gabriel said, He makes me itchy hanging on me like he does with his shitty Southern accent and his shitty Southern ways.

You've got an accent of your own, I told him. Fernstermaker's is only broader. He can't help it that he's so dumb he thinks you're a Latter Day Saint.

Screw him, Gabriel said. I wish he'd get off my back and leave us alone.

Us? I said, my eyes popping. Why *us*?

Oh, he's always wanting to have lunch with us or walk home with us.

It's you, I told him. It's YOU.

Well, yeah, but then you're so nice to him, always talking to him and taking up for him and laughing at his stupid jokes.

I said, I would never have believed it (and I would not have) but you are jealous of an eighteen-year-old infant.

SO? Gabriel said angrily. I got a right to be. You said we couldn't talk about your husband and we never mention his sacred fucking name. I guess I got a right to be jealous of somebody and Fernstermaker is it.

For maybe one whole minute I puzzled on it. G. was jealous of J. and using Fernstermaker as a substitute? Using F. was crazy enough but the really crazy thing was being jealous at all when Gabriel has everything (assuming . . . oh fatuous assumption . . . that having me is everything) and J. has nothing.

That guy, Gabriel went on, that fat-ass husband of yours has everything and I got nothing. There he sits, having a full-course meal and what do I get? The leavings from Whitey's table.

I was so shocked I couldn't open my mouth. We were going up the stairs to his room by then and when we went in I just dropped into a chair at the table and sat staring at him.

OK, OK, he said, throwing his books on the table. So I'm a bastard. Didn't you ever think all that life you got over there with that big fat slob in that big fat house might be on my mind sometimes?

What's going on (I said) when you think of my husband as Whitey and me as a crumb from his table? I mean, what am I and what are you?

I don't know, he said, walking angrily around the room. It's that mothering Fernstermaker that's done it. Seeing him so white and Southern sucking up to you . . .

You're crazy! It's not even to me.

I'm just something for his frigging conscience, the Madman said. It's you he feels right with. There he is, every goddamned day, with his long white face hanging out and you talking and laughing with him like you and he belonged together and I'm just somebody's house nigger. No, I'm not even IN the house.

I stared at him and muttered, Oh Boy Oh Boy Oh Boy.

Well? he said, looking furiously at me. Isn't it true?

And suddenly I started to laugh. It was so crazy it was funny. Here was Gabriel feeling like an outsider, a nigger, when everything was all the other way. People are so insane I do seriously wonder how the H. race has survived this long.

What's so fucking funny? he said, still angry.

Gabriel, I said, *I* am the nigger that's not even in the house. I am an old creep, looking from the outside at your world. Don't you think that sometimes *I* feel like the outsider, the one who catches the crumbs, stuck as I am in my fat old house in my fat old world? And, as for the black-white crap, well, if you're a nigger, I'm a nigger or if I'm Whitey so are you. You know that.

He slowly circled the room for a minute, then he said that about the color he was off the beam. But he said he did get this feeling he was left out of everything important in my life and somehow Fernstermaker seemed to just BE all that he was left out of.

Then he sat down across from me and he said, You're right, Sophie, *we* don't have any color but whenever I think of that man you're married to I see him like big and fat and dumb and white, a Southern white sheriff, you know?

I groaned, feeling bad for J. and this slander on him, yet I could see how Gabriel felt. I told him I did know but J. was not fat nor dumb and not at all like a white sheriff. But I can't (I said) talk about him. You can see why, can't you? It would be wrong and I'd feel like a Whore and a Judas and it wouldn't do us any good. But I'll tell you this, the life we have here is the important life to me and this is where I most belong.

And then, although I assumed he knew it, I said sort of offhandedly, And if it makes any difference to you, I don't sleep with him.

I wasn't thinking just of that, he said.

But he looked so enormously relieved that I realized he had been thinking a great deal of that. And I said I had thought the one man–one woman stuff was out the window what with the communes and all.

This ain't no commune, baby, he said. This here's my castle.

Later, we were in bed and I sat up and asked him to scratch an itch on my back. When he couldn't seem to find the place, I said, You're not much good as a house nigger, you know that, Fernstermaker?

He laughed and then lying back he said sort of meditatively, I guess I have been kind of mean to old Fernstermaker. And then (oh, the transparent sweet childishness of him) he said, I am going to be so nice to Fernstermaker he won't know what hit him.

Sometimes I do not know how we are all going to overcome. Here's Gabriel to whom I feel closer than anybody and he makes up these stereotypes of house nigger and Whitey's table and all that. Even jealous as he was, it was a pretty far out (and low down) way for him to think. Suppose I'd taken it seriously, as I might have done, would he have gone on with it? If he had stuck to it, would we have separated, each of us then being sure that never the twain shall meet? That word . . . twain . . . now I think of it I've never been sure what it means. Must look it up.

It means TWO. Nothing more or less. I always thought it meant race or genre. I am really awfully ignorant. Maybe I'll go back to school one day. I might get a Ph.D. and BE something. But what would I want to be?

One thing I know I will never be is a psychiatric social worker. But every third female seems to be or be becoming one. There's Deb now in her second year. And sometimes as I sit listening to her (as I did last night after she called and asked if she could come by), my eyes glazing over as she goes on about how hard it is to understand how she could've been so deceived by Marsden. . . . Well, she is my friend and I won't say more than that I wonder sometimes.

And the other day at a cocktail party J. said we had to go to, I ran into Mary Anne Hodges whom I haven't seen in a long time. She has just become a social worker and is doing guidance at one of the loony bins.

I asked her about it but all she wanted to talk about was her kitchen which is being redone. Her big problem about which she talked non-stop is whether to have a gas or elec. stove. She hesitates, she told me, to have elec. even though it is cleaner because of possible black-outs or brown-outs. I advised her to get both gas and elec. and she said perfectly seriously that I might have something there.

I can remember when Mary Anne and Harold gave parties at which we'd dance half the night and how lively and funny she was when we worked together for Stevenson.

Oh yes, I almost forgot her parting shot(s). She said I really ought to get out and do something. You're stagnating (she said). You simply don't realize it until you get out and see the world. I tell you, Sophie, it's absolutely saved my mind.

I felt like telling her it might've saved her mind but it has done so by shrinking it to the size of a pea.

And this is the wonderful world Gabriel is left out of!

I keep having the feeling of things going more and more awry . . . the heavy small-mindedness of Mary Anne the other day, the eternal tedium of Deb telling her memory beads, the flat opaqueness of J., the madness of Gabriel and his nigger and Whitey. And, of course, it is not just my world that is a mess. There are the very real facts of the war, the arms race, the retreat from integration. To have to get up every day with the knowledge that Nixon is still there (and that one cannot hope that he is not since then there would be Agnew who is, if possible, worse) that alone is enough to shrivel the soul.

Saturday, Dec. 13

J. at an all-day–all-evening meeting so I had a long time with Gabriel. It was cold but beautiful and we went for a walk down by the ice-skating rink. The music was playing and Gabriel said it looked like fun and he wished he knew how. I said I was sure he'd find it easy so we got the car and drove to the house where I got my skates and J.'s (I felt funny about that but I figured with all the more important things I have given or loaned Gabriel that are rightfully J.'s . . . and not just physical things . . . it was foolish to quibble over a pair of skates). They fit fine so we went back to the rink.

He was, as I'd thought he'd be, quick to learn. He's wonderfully well-coordinated and it was fun to skate around together. It was also nice to feel for once with him that I am a competent, capable person (I am a good skater, though I say it who shouldn't).

I said something of this when we were back in the room in bed with our sides welded together and my right hand in his left. I said it was a nice feeling I had there at the rink, where I had been the insider who knew the ropes and was able, not so much to show them to him, but to show him that I knew them.

He looked puzzled and asked me what I was talking

about. It was (still is) important to me but I never did make it clear to him and maybe not to myself either.

I so often feel (I told him) that I'm trailing along with you, running to keep up. Maybe it comes back to that business we were talking about of this being your world and my feeling that I am out of it by reason of age, sex and previous condition of servitude. I don't mean the house nigger business.

He interrupted to say he thought I DID mean the nigger business. Whenever you say anything about age I know it means nigger to you, he said. When are you going to wake up and see you're not an old lady but a fine, beautiful girl?

I could feel myself getting hot all over and I guess I must have actually reddened because Gabriel laughed.

How old you say you are? he asked poking me in the ribs.

Old enough not to believe everything I hear, I said. Then I said I knew I was not homely but beautiful is something else. Beautiful (I said) is that. And I pointed to the photograph thumbtacked to the wall at the foot of the bed.

It was of a truly beautiful girl. Young, dark, thin with high cheekbones, large deep black eyes, black hair skinned back and falling to her shoulders in a great smoky cloud. She was wearing trousers and a sweat shirt and she looked like the queen of some ancient Golden Civilization. She had been there ever since I first came to the room and I had wondered about her. Since Thanksgiving I had wondered more. I had wanted to ask about her but somehow I never felt sufficiently easy (or confident) to ask what might seem prying, jealous questions. Today I did not feel prying or jealous and it seemed all right.

Gabriel glanced at the picture and said, Oh her. Then he crawled to the foot of the bed, pulled the photograph down and let it drop on the floor.

I forgot she was there, he said as he got back under the covers. Else I would've taken her down before.

Where is she? I asked.

In jail probably.

She was your girl? (It's odd how easy it was to ask him these things. But then everything is easy with him.)

I guess she was as much mine as she'll ever be anybody's. And then he sighed, a soul-deep sigh.

I had turned over on my stomach and was propped up on my elbows so I could see his face which looked remembering. I didn't say anything but I was hoping he'd remember out loud.

I just about blew my mind over that girl, he said, looking up at the ceiling. She was, well, hard isn't the word but it'll do. She was always a driving kind of person, even at the beginning when we were in the SDS together. Then, after the Chicago hassle, I sort of fell away. Like after it split up there wasn't much left in it, not for me anyway. She went on into the Weathermen and we still hung out together but she was all the time busy lifting canned goods and underwear and stuff for the revolution. She was busted a couple of times but she got off on both of them. Then she got like sour on the Weathermen and moved on to the Panthers. She used to beat up on me because I wasn't about to become a Panther. Called me St. Thomas of the Assholes. Man! (he kind of laughed but not really). I don't know why I kept hanging in there with her so long. Am I dumb or what, Sophie?

I told him No, he was not dumb only a masochistic slob. And I prodded him to go on.

Well, I managed to last through the Panthers but then she changed signals on me and went into Women's Lib and that did us in. Could you believe it? She wouldn't come to bed without she had delivered me a lecture on male chauvinism and by that time my balls were so froze up I didn't have anything male left. One thing you got to say (he said smiling), if Women's Lib wins out they will sure stop the population explosion. Nobody will even be able to screw, let alone want to.

Fernstermaker, you are sounding very reactionary (I said and I was not really joking). Women have been more depressed and for longer than anybody and we need to be liberated.

Everybody needs to be liberated, he said cheerfully. But no use to liberate one group at the expense of another. I mean, how come the ladies got to rise by tromping on my balls?

He has a funny way of saying things and that made me laugh. Then he said sort of meditatively, Funny, I don't mind you calling me Fernstermaker.

Why should you? You don't mind Fernstermaker, I said.

He agreed that he didn't. But he's no soul brother, he said, and I guess I won't ever like his molasses accent.

I said it seemed to me it depended on what the voice said not the accent which said it.

You call me saintly, he said. But you don't care about accents and I got a real hang-up on white Southern talk.

Yes, but you don't hate people and I do.

Where you get that idea? he said. Certainly I hate people. But just certain ones. When I was a kid, back in Birmingham, I thought I really hated all people and especially whites.

And he told me this story. I could see he was back there in it because his accent got more and more Southern as he told it.

It was September of 1963 and he was a kid in high school in Birmingham. There was the bombing of the black church in which 4 little black girls were killed and there was the riot.

Hate? he said, I hated everybody that day. Not just whites but the dumb niggers who sat and prayed and let this happen. It was that day I gave up on God, never did get Him back but never mind that.

He and some other kids were tromping through the streets, not causing any violence because they had nothing to do violence with, when they were set upon by some cops. Gabriel received the particular attention of a big, fat white slob (NB: J. as the white Southern sheriff) who kicked him in the balls and when he fell hit him over the head. They, Gabriel and the others, were thrown into the Black Maria and hauled off to jail where they were packed into a cell so crowded that "when somebody had to piss there wasn't hardly enough room to open his pants." He went in hating and he came out hating even worse.

His father (a Baptist minister, follower of Dr. King's, dead now) tried to get Gabriel back to the church.

But Gabriel hated the old man then, hated the church and was just biding his time till he could get away. "Out of the whole damn, cotton-picking, Jesus-ridden, woolly-headed mess."

Then that summer he went out to the back country with some other kids, some blacks and some whites down from the north, on a voter registration drive. And there he saw what he, a city boy, raised by comparatively educated parents, had never seen before. "Back-country niggers, niggers so poor in mind and body and spirit they were afraid to talk to us, niggers so beat down and dumb they didn't know what the vote was."

And it came to me (he said) that there wasn't any way in the world that bombs or guns could raise those people up. Even if we had the bombs and the guns, what good would the revolution be to people who hardly knew how to use toilet paper, not to speak of pen or pencil? They got to be taught. They got to learn what the choices are before they can make them. It was that summer I made up my mind I would go away and learn and I would come back and teach them about voting and pens and pencils and toilet paper and everything else they got to know.

Sonny Boy, I said (and my voice cracked with the effort to keep from crying), now that Dr. King is gone, you are the last humanist. But his death was the end. The end for people like him and like you. There's no room for you anymore.

He shook his head. Where I'm at (he said) there's nothing BUT room. You watch, Sophie, there's going to be a change, not back to what was, but on past what is. I'll find more like me and I'll drag them south and I'll take and shove the young out and then grab them back when they're ready.

Had we but world enough and time Gabriel's plans might work but I am afraid that the world and time are running out. But, I can offer nothing better and I am, anyway, coming to reject the idea that there is any one right way to anything. Maybe all salvation is individual and consists of doing one's thing. Which is maybe what Voltaire meant by *Il faut cultiver notre jardin.*

We started supper (J. was to have dinner at the

club with the other people at the meeting) and we talked some more about Gabriel's plans. Rosenblum (his adviser) has said he will try to fix him up with something in a black college when his thesis is done.

I asked where he'd like to go if he could choose. All the while we were talking I felt a chill falling on me at the thought of his leaving. And, as if he felt it too, Gabriel said it was such a long time in the future he hadn't thought about it, wasn't going to think about it.

I went home around nine to find J. slopping disconsolately about the kitchen. The dinner meeting had been canceled and he was feeling put-upon because he had had to make a sandwich and eat it alone. As he complained about eating alone, I wondered (silently) if he has ever given a thought to the thousands of sandwiches I have fixed and eaten by myself.

Nevertheless my guilt drove me to make him another sandwich and some coffee and to defrost some cheese cake. While he was eating I sat across from him and opened the mail.

He asked where I'd been and I said I had had dinner with a friend from the Center.

I thought they were all so young, he said.

So? I said.

Nothing, he said. I just thought they might be a little young for you.

I didn't answer as I came upon a letter from the White House. It was supposedly in response to a letter of mine calling Nixon to task for his reversal on school integration. But it wasn't a response; it was just a collection of words saying, in effect, the President knows better than you so why don't you shut your face?

I read it to J. and then I ran my finger over *The*

White House and I said, Why, it isn't engraved! It isn't even raised printing.

J. laughed and said the President's stationery was one thing he was not going to worry about.

I said no, but it was disgusting just the same. Just what one might expect (I said) of his cheap, low-grade mind.

I should think the contents are better evidence of that than the paper, J. said.

That too, I said. But the letter's about what I expected. Except he might've said something about the Republican Party. I wrote quite a lot about the damage he's doing Our Party.

OUR party? J. said. But you're not a Republican.

No, I said. But when I write to Fat-Face I always say I am.

J. looked positively stern as he told me that it was dishonest of me to pose as a Republican when I am about as far from it as one can get.

Why, you'd think it was a moral issue, I said, amazed at him. After all, I could very well be a Republican. If I could vote for John Lindsay I would, and I did vote for Brooke. Anyway, while I'm writing the letters I *feel* like a Republican.

But you're not, J. said, still with that schoolmasterly air. And that kind of thing is infantile.

So I'm infantile, I snapped. Maybe that's why I get on so well with the infants at the Center.

Then J. exploded in a kind of all-purpose anger. How do we get into these things? he wanted to know. I didn't (he said) mean to attack you. Why do we always end in some kind of pointless disagreement?

I wanted to tell him that I thought it is because we each have a great resentment against the other but just then the deus ex machina rang and it was for him and he got a sheaf of papers and sat down with old Tom or Dick or Whoever.

I put in some laundry and cleaned up the mess he had made with his one sandwich. Then when he was finally off the phone it was time for the 11:00 news (never send to ask for whom the news tolls, it tolls for J.) and when that was over he sighed and said he had to catch an eight a.m. plane and he was going to bed.

I nodded and didn't bother to ask where he was going nor when he'd be back. Then, standing half in the room and half in the hall, he said, Not that it matters, I suppose, but I'll be back tomorrow night.

He looked so tired and defeated sagging against the door jamb that I felt sorry (and of course guilty) that I can do nothing to help him.

I'm sorry, J., I said. I am really and truly sorry I am such a lousy wife. You deserve better.

He seemed to sag even more. Then he straightened up and said, People generally get what they ask for.

Then he dragged his poor puritanical ass up the stairs.

Sometimes these last weeks, I have felt as if there is an enormous box in which I have shut and locked a number of problems which I will one day have to look at. But tonight, as J. plodded up the stairs, I had the terrible feeling that I have locked HIM in the box and I wanted to go after him and say something, something kind and good that would let him out of that box.

But I cannot face what that would lead to so I went

back to the kitchen and put the clothes in the dryer. I am a compulsive clothes-washer these days and I do not need any Ass Bird to tell me why.

Monday, Dec. 15

Tonight at dinner I made a half-hearted attempt to tell J. about Gabriel. I try to be halfway (if not pathologically) honest with myself but I truly do not know if I really wanted to tell him or if I only wanted to kid myself that I had tried and failed. I expect it was the latter and that I did it so I could continue to deceive J. and not feel so bad about it.

Because it is a deception and I am uncomfortable about it these days. I know perfectly well that one day Gabriel and I have to end but I know too that I am not going to stop seeing him until I have to. What I don't know is where J. is in all this. I do feel something for him, but I would be hard put to say what it is. I do not even know if I want to leave him now or ever. But certainly, for now, for as long as I have Gabriel I have left J. in every way that counts.

I served our solitary dinner early so I could get in with my tale before the news came on at 6:30. When the children were home there was an absolute rule of no TV during meals but since Ames left, J. has taken to listening to Chuntley and Buntley throughout the meal. I tried having dinner later but he doesn't like that and we cannot eat any earlier because he isn't home.

I started by telling him I knew our life together was

not much of a life and not together and that it was as much my fault as his (I am not at all sure that that last statement is true but I was, I think, assuming this lesser guilt because of my very real larger one).

J. said that was very generous of me.

His voice was so cold and unforthcoming that I almost lost heart but I plowed on and said I knew the absence of sex relations (why do I so dislike phrases like that? Why do I use them?) must he hard on him unless he had somebody else and I hoped he had.

At this point he got up and turned on the TV and then he sat back down and said (one eye on the TV and the other on his plate) that was *too* generous of me.

I asked him if we could turn the TV off.

He said if I was trying to tell him I was working through a fantasy and he should leave me alone, I could save my breath. He said Ass Bird had already told him and he would abide by the doctor's opinion and could he please now listen to the news?

I waited until the commercial and then I turned the sound down and I asked him what he would say if I told him it was not a fantasy love affair but a real one.

He said he wouldn't believe it.

Why not? I asked.

Because (he said) you are incapable of dissembling and also because you simply don't accept sex that way.

What way? I asked.

On a part-time, purely physical basis, he said. And then he said, And as for me finding someone else, I'll arrange my own life, thank you, and I don't need your advice.

Then he turned the sound back on and I gave up.

I didn't tell J. but my last session with Ass Bird was just that. As soon as I came in, even before I sat down, I told him.

I am giving you a Xmas present, I said.

AB was edging his chair further back from his desk (and thus further from me) and as he gave a final shove with his rear, he said, HUMPH? What's that? Then with an expression on his face which I could not decipher he said I mustn't do that.

I said it wasn't worth making any fuss about as it was a very small present. It is only (I said) that you will be relieved of me after today. I am taking my custom elsewhere.

He lost his footing on the open desk drawer where he keeps his big fat foot perched and he almost fell out of his big black chair. What do you MEAN? he screeched in a most unanalytical way.

I mean, I said, that I am putting my head in other hands.

I don't know why AB has always driven me to say things like that, things I never mean to say, things that just pop into my head, things that don't make too much sense actually.

What do you mean "other hands"? he demanded.

I said I had read about this therapy-by-mail course and as it was being offered at a Big Reduction I thought I'd try it.

Another of your jokes, he said, looking both relieved and annoyed.

It wasn't very funny, was it? I said. And that's one of the reasons I'm leaving. I don't like feeling that I'm boring you all the time.

Why, he wanted to know, did I feel I bored him?

I said because he was always yawning.

He said yawning was not, contrary to popular belief, a sign of boredom but was due to lack of oxygen.

Well, then, I said, I don't like feeling I'm using up all your oxygen. Whatever it is, I know you find me and my problems pretty dim-witted and I, in turn, don't feel you are exactly the Seven Pillars of Wisdom.

He interrupted to say that was because of my low self-esteem and because I had not worked through my hostility to him.

I told him my self-esteem had got less in the time I had spent with him and that life was too short for me to work through my hostility to him.

He then said quite a lot about me being in a danger-out state with my fantasies. I said I had told him the truth and if he did not believe me that was his problem.

He rubbed his forehead and he looked hot and sweaty and, for once, almost human as he said my child-like transparency made it very difficult to know when to take me seriously.

I forbore to say that I was obviously not so childish nor so transparent if he could not tell when I was serious and when not. I just kept my mouth shut while he droned on and on about my terrible repressions (that I can't remember that I masturbated), my hostilities (to him, mainly), and my fantasies about a lover.

It was not a pleasant session and I was glad when he finally got up and told me very coldly to remember the door is always open. Even speaking metaphorically, that is a joke. There are *two* doors, one right behind the other; both are lined with some heavy carpeting and both are opened (and closed) very guardedly by AB in a manner which makes me think of Bluebeard and his Secret Room.

I suppose he means well and maybe if I had never known good, wise Dr. Damon I would've been able to get on with him. No, what kind of crap is that? AB is totally unfitted for his line of work and I would never have got on with him no matter where I met him nor under what circumstances.

Tuesday, Dec. 16

Today at the Center. People are still streaming in trying to find out everything about the Draft Lottery. We have written answers to some of the most frequently asked questions and have posted a calendar which gives all the draft priority numbers with birth dates. But knowing where you are in the Lottery doesn't say anything definite about where you actually will end up. Some draft boards are saying that if the calls stay high, men with 366 will be drafted. The Pentagon says the last third are probably safe but of course nobody in his right mind would believe anything the Pentagon says.

Most times at the Center I do my job in a rational, matter-of-fact way but sometimes when I think of what it is that we are working against, this war, the nightmare of this seemingly unendable obscenity sweeps over me and it is all I can do to keep from rushing screaming into the street. Today was one of those days and although I did what I had to do I was feeling very uptight.

Gabriel came in at lunchtime and we ate sandwiches which I had brought. Things slackened in the early afternoon and Gabriel, who also seemed sort of uptight, wanted to cut out so we left.

He wanted to get out someplace and I suggested the Arboretum or the Mt. Auburn Cemetery where we walk sometimes. But he wanted to really get out, he said. And finally he said, Let's go to Ipswich.

You mean the beach? I said incredulously.

He said he did.

I reminded him that there was snow on the ground and that it was COLD.

He said, Let's go anyway, so I said OK and we got in the car and set out. We sang most of the way and by the time we got there I was out of my slough and he seemed to be in good spirits.

The beach was of course deserted. And it was cold and snowy and windy but it was exhilarating and we ran up the beach and yelled into the wind. We were sitting up on a dune huddled together, when Gabriel kissed me and in a minute I realized we were on the Royal Road to Screwing. I started to demur because it was too cold, or too wet or too something, and then I thought how insane it was to refuse any part of this beneficence for any reason whatsoever and I relaxed and welcomed it.

Afterwards I took off my skirt and pantihose and waded in, in my boots, and dipped my bottom in the water. As I was squatting there, screaming at the fierce cold and Gabriel was laughing, I thought how much Gabriel has done for this woman's liberation. A month ago I would've died before I would've let anybody see me in such a position.

Gabriel wanted to get some food and come back but it was too late and I had to go home. He didn't like that and he was silent and withdrawn as we started back. I knew it was because we had to go, or rather because my big fat life made me have to go, and I said I was sorry and that one day soon we'd plan ahead and come out and spend the whole day.

He sort of shrugged and said that wasn't any answer.

I asked him what was the question.

And he said the question was how we could keep on living this crazy life.

I felt all the blood drain right out of me and I said there was no law that said we had to keep on.

He said coldly to cut the crap; that that was no answer either and I knew it.

I just sat there trying to put a shell over me so as not to see or hear anything, most of all not to feel or think anything. Like what happens to some forms of life, I don't know which, when they encyst over and nothing can touch them.

He didn't say anything more until we were almost back to Boston. Then he reached over and took my hand (which had been lying like a fish out of water in my lap) and said, with what sounded like cheerfulness, Never mind, crazy or not, it's a good life we've got.

I knew he was talking more to himself than to me but I agreed that it was so.

When we stopped at his place he held me and with his cheek next to mine, he said, Would you believe love, Sophie?

Fortunately he couldn't see my face so he didn't see the tears that sprang to my eyes. I only laughed and kissed him and then I pushed him out and said I'd come over early tomorrow.

Driving home I tried to encyst over again so I would not think about "Would you believe love?" It is the first time that word has ever been mentioned between us and it wrenches me all over again as I write it. I got home in some kind of shape to find J. pacing furiously up and down the living room. As soon as I walked in he said, Where have you been? We're late and . . . my God! . . . what've you been doing? You've got sand all over you. What the HELL have you been doing?

I said I would be ready in a minute and what were we late for?

Good God, don't you remember anything anymore? he demanded. We're supposed to be co-hosts for that reception for the Israelis.

I dashed upstairs and I was ready in only about ten minutes and we were *not* late for the damn Reception. The Lesters (another of the co-hosts, there were at least a half dozen of us co-sic-hosts) came in the door with us. It was at the Faculty Club and, like most affairs of that kind, full of agreeable people being agreeable and leaving me with a feeling of emptiness and pointlessness.

There was one small exchange which was *not* agreeable and which added gloom to the emptiness.

It was with Ethel Graham. She and I have never been really friendly since the time we worked on a civil liberties thing of which she was chairman. She was a good chairman but pretty much of a slave driver, always saying things like "Is that ALL you've done? Goodness, I thought we'd have those out of the way by now." And, "Sophie (or Mary or Susie) would you drop this off at the printers' on your way home, and while you're at it would you stop at the post office and mail these and pick up another roll of stamps and, oh yes, why don't you take these packages along." She was a real garbage-dumper.

One day when I was at the airport I noticed the basket of Avis buttons and I took a handful and I lettered a "PLEASE!" above the We Try Harder. The next day we (her committee) all wore them. It was supposed to be a joke but Ethel said coldly, Where did you get THOSE? and when I said I had donated them, she gave me quite a dirty look and did not speak to me for some time.

Anyway, at the Reception she was talking about why blacks want separate black houses. She said it was because "they" were taken from nothing and had finally made the country club "so to speak" and now were uncomfortable. Poor lambs (she said) it's only what you'd expect. We've been forced to move too fast for them.

She also said quite a little bit about people "who come from ghettos and miss their soul food and don't know which fork to use, so to speak." And how they are more at ease with "their own kind."

I said I did not think it was a matter of manners or soul food. If it were just a sense of social inferiority then why hadn't the children of Jewish immigrants, the ghetto kids of another era, formed *themselves* into separate enclaves so they could have their kosher soul food and eat it with their feet if they wanted to.

Ethel said it was not the same thing at all.

I asked her to tell me the difference, aside from color.

She said the Jews always had an intellectual tradition and were used to "things of the mind."

I said things of the mind didn't help much with fish forks and that her argument had been based on coming from a socially, not intellectually, lower background.

She said, Well, she meant intellectually too. And how it was a "whole complex" and went on to give a long history of the Jews which had nothing, so far as I could see, to do with the price of eggs.

It was a stupid argument and I wished I had not opened my mouth. But that is so often the case with me.

I either open my mouth and wish I had not or I do not open it and wish to Christ I had.

Afterwards, on the way to the car, I said to J. that I thought Ethel Graham was a very silly woman and what did he think?

He said he didn't know her.

I said of course he did; that we had only known the Grahams for maybe 20 thousand years.

Nevertheless, he said, *I don't know Ethel Graham.* Not well enough, anyway, to know whether she's silly.

I muttered that he didn't know much.

He asked what I'd said. And as I stumbled over some icy mounds, I said loudly, I said, Now is the winter of my discontent.

Then he said, If you'd wear your boots it wouldn't be so bad.

In the car, I sat in a physical and mental slump, just barely holding myself together until I would be home and could get off by myself.

But then J. said, Let's stop in at the Wursthaus and grab a sandwich. And I cringed and felt I really could not hold myself up much longer.

I know you don't like it, he said. But it's quick and we haven't much time.

I asked why we didn't have much time.

He said there was to be an informal get-together with the Israelis at the Somebody's House after dinner. I said he would have to count me out as I had Xmas packages to do.

Then during the wait for the quick service, he asked what I had been doing earlier to get wet and sandy.

I said I had been cleaning up a beach.

With those people at the Center? he asked. And I

nodded (a nod does not somehow seem so much of a lie as an actual word).

He said this seemed an odd time to do it. And that I certainly did get into some funny things with those Center people.

I allowed as how that was so.

And all evening as I've been wrapping and packing I've been thinking of this very funny thing I've got into.

I am torn between joy that Gabriel loves me (and wants to say so) and guilt and confusion because he is beginning to want more for us than we can ever have. We are not just the Odd couple, we are the Impossible couple. By any objective criteria we have nothing going for us at all.

But we have so much! How can I be rational, moral and upright and end this thing which fills me, surrounds me, warms me, delights me (and which, I think, does the same for Gabriel). Every day seems like my birthday, special and loving and happy (even when we are sad we are somehow basically happy inside ourselves). The very knowledge that he is there is like a warm cloak in which I am wrapped, the thought of him is a magic lamp which seems, almost literally, to warm my heart.

I know it cannot be *wrong* to feel these things. They are the best and most human of emotions. When the thesis is done Gabriel will leave and go back south. When that day comes we will have to end but it has not yet come and I will keep what I have while I can have it.

Wednesday, Dec. 17

Went over early to Gabriel's. He wasn't there and I did some typing of what looked to be thesis material. Lately, he does not leave his notes out where I can find them. I must ask him about this.

He came in after a while. Said he'd been having a conf. with Rosenblum.

We talked about Xmas. He said he wanted to give me a present and what did I want. I said I did not want anything and over his strong protests I made him swear he would not give me one single thing. I told him that if we could not have a real Xmas together (which we cannot since I must be home) I didn't want a play-acting one.

He said, You going to try to do me out of my Xmas Tree? Why, Sophie-girl, you can't do that. I always have a tree.

I didn't want us to have a tree but I could not do him out of his tree so I said sure if he wanted a tree, we would have one.

We had lunch and then went around looking for a tree but everything was too expensive or too ugly. We decided to go to the Haymarket tomorrow and get one there.

Back at the room and his friend Sam came in. Gabriel asked Sam something about his group at Brandeis. I have never been able to understand just what kind of group this is and whenever I have asked, Sam has given the kind of put-down answer that doesn't explain anything. The group is wholly black, that much is clear, and it is activist and separatist but they are not Panthers. Sam didn't say much; just that things were moving.

Later Gabriel was arguing with him about black dorms and cited something Julian Bond had said against separation.

Sam said Julian Bond was a dead cat. Gabriel laughed and said that was just what he was afraid Sam was going to become if he kept on.

The way Sam's face closed up and he glanced at me as he changed the subject made me feel as if he thinks I'm a CIA agent. I still like Sam although he doesn't (I think) like *me* anymore. He did at the beginning, I'm pretty sure, and the falling off is due (I do believe) not to anything I have said or done but to the worsening climate everywhere.

A climate which certainly obtains at home these days. There is a wall of concrete blocks between J. and me; a wall which does not however insulate me from a feeling of loss and sadness. It comes over me from time to time and I see us as if I were looking through a telescope from a long way off. We move around the house, carefully separated as if we had invisible plastic covers, not speaking much, avoiding contact, almost never looking at each other.

We had to go to some damn party. I wanted to beg off but J. seemed to want me to go so I did, feeling that I must not let him down *everywhere.*

It was the usual, with all the people who drink too much busy drinking too much and I felt so unhappy and bored (is there anybody in the world who really likes cocktail parties?) that I drank 4 or 5 cups of eggnog to try to cheer up but it only made me feel sick. We had been asked to stay for a buffet supper but somewhere around 7:00 my stomach began to feel funny so I told J. I would get a ride with some people who were leaving and I came on home.

I've taken a couple of aspirin but I still feel queasy, uneasy. It is probably nothing to do with the egg nog and not in my stomach but my head, or what passes for a head. I am anxious and sad and guilty about Gabriel as well as J. It is Christmas which shows me all too clearly that I am living two irreconcilable lives and not meeting the needs of either of them.

Thursday, Dec. 18

Up and out of the house early. Did the marketing and some more Xmas shopping, cleaned the house a bit and hurried off to Gabriel's. My queasy stomach had seemed much better but by the time I got to his place it felt funny again. Not funny enough to bother about, though, so we went on down to the Haymarket to look for the tree.

We found a nice one, small and well-shaped but not, of course, very cheap. Nothing is cheap anymore.

He was in a great mood, joking and laughing, and I tried to keep my end (or rather my head) up. We went to this place we've been before . . . a leather-goods shop run by a very nice guy named Harold . . . and Gabriel insisted on buying me a belt. Said it was NOT a Xmas present and would I please be a good girl and not give him any lip. So I accepted, gracefully I hope, and wore the belt and felt proud of myself that I did not try to give him anything in return.

We bought some groceries and at the fish place the

man gave us some raw clams which tasted good at the time but did not seem like a good idea a little later when we went to a pizza parlor for lunch. My stomach had that terribly important feeling that stomachs get when something is wrong with them. Finally, I had to tell him I had to go home. It was not, by then, just my stomach but my intestines as well. Everything was roiling around inside and I felt like Vesuvius getting ready to erupt.

We just made it to the room and I did erupt. Got to the john in time to vomit and had no sooner finished that when the intestines started and I had to sit down and empty them.

Finally, after a little more heaving, it all let up and I lay on the bed and Gabriel put a cold wet washcloth on my head. He was so *good.* I would never have believed a man could be so good around a sick person. J. just takes flight, says CALL THE DOCTOR! and runs as if the hounds of hell were after him. Gabriel held my head over the bowl (just the way I used to do with the children) and wiped my mouth and handed me a glass of water to rinse with.

I knew it was just one of the bugs, whichever one is going around right now, and would be over soon and there was nothing to do for it. But Gabriel wanted to do something so I remembered I used to give the kids Coke and I told him he could get some. He did and I drank it and as he went around putting clothes away and neatening up things, he said I should not worry about the Xmas tree, that he would do it himself and surprise me.

Then after a little, he said, And don't worry about what I said the other day, about this crazy life. I know you can't do anything now about the bind you're in and we're not going to mess up all we got because I want more. So I just want to say forget it. OK?

It is not possible to say how grateful I felt to him for that; nor how it touched me. I wanted to tell him but I couldn't find any words so I asked him if he would feel like coming to bed with a bug-riddled body.

He said was I sure I felt like it. I said I was positive. So he did and it was gentle and kind of quiet, as if somehow this were part of the treatment (which it was, I guess) and I felt so cared for, in every sense, that it was as if I had had some miraculous cure.

Before I left we tried to get some kind of schedule for the next few days. He has the Roxbury party and something at Rosenblum's tomorrow night and something with Sam at Brandeis on Sat. There is the party at the Center sometime next week. I forget when. And I have the Blind School party and there are any number of things J. and I are supposed to go to not all of which I can get out of.

Gabriel kept saying I should stay in bed this weekend and not try to do anything at all. But I said I was sure to be all right tomorrow and I would see him at the Center.

Home to hear the phone ringing and it was J., annoyed because he'd tried to get me all day to tell me he was planning to bring 2 people home to dinner.

I suppose it's late for that now, he said sounding aggrieved.

I said No, if it was only two I could manage.

Then he said that some people would be coming over afterwards for a meeting. Nothing big (he said). Only a half-dozen or so . . . we're going to talk about the

London conference. Just be sure there's enough to drink.

So I rustled around, getting stuff out of the freezer and calling the liquor store for a quick delivery. I was setting the table when the bug struck again.

I remembered paregoric which I used to use in diarrhea emergencies with the children so I took some. Whether that did the trick I don't know but something did and I was OK when J. appeared with his 2 gents and OK during dinner.

Afterwards when the meeting began I excused myself and came up here.

I am writing this in bed thinking how good it was this afternoon to be cared for. No one has held my head or put a cloth on it since I was a child (although I've certainly vomited since then). Indeed, except for when I had the children, I don't think I have ever felt that anybody was taking care of me. I'm sure Cissy, that old Voice of Reason, would say, Why should anybody take care of you? You're grown and perfectly capable of taking care of yourself.

And I am and I do. But what's so bad about liking to be cared for sometimes? Seems to me I do it for other people. If J. says he has a headache I don't say, Go take an aspirin. I *bring* him an aspirin and a glass of water. If he will admit he's sick (which he almost never does), I try to persuade him to stay home and I call the Univ. and I bring him his papers and the lapboard and I come, silently, with things to eat and drink. I keep people off his neck and I avoid hanging around him myself.

But when I am sick (which I try never to be and seldom am) it is really Sauve Qui Peut around here. J. makes for the life boats, leaving me to scramble around with such help as I can get from Mrs. K. (if it is her

"Day"), Sage's grocery delivery, and the kids. When Ames is home she has always helped me. But if I were ever so sick I could not get out of bed and Ames were *not* here, I believe I would be left to rot in the guest room (where I go when I am really sick) and would not be found until Mrs. K. came to clean.

These are not complaints I could ever voice to anybody because it all sounds so self-laudatory (see how much I do for other people) and so self-pitying (see how little is done for me). But it seems to me that, until Gabriel, nobody in my adult life ever cared for me. In the sense that I am talking about. Now I have that TLC in Gabriel and it sometimes frightens me to realize how much I depend on it. And on him. He cares about me as somebody to sleep with but also he cares about ME. He makes me feel wanted, needed and something else. I guess the word is cherished.

That is certainly the way I feel about him. Sometimes I think it is too much, that I have no right to so much. Then I remember that in fact I do not have any right and I wonder how much longer it will be permitted to me.

Sunday, Dec. 21

The weekend has been mostly but not completely grim. Haven't seen Gabriel since Thurs. and the damn bug kept gnawing, but both children were home today and that was an unexpected good.

Fri. to the Square to get things for the Blind School party and was seized several times in the Coop with cramps. Managed to finish shopping and get home before the diarrhea struck again. In between trips to the john I got some presents wrapped.

Was in my (the guest) room lying on the bed when J. came home and stuck his head in and asked what was the matter with me.

I said I didn't feel good. He said we were supposed to go to dinner at the Somebody's and was I going?

I said No, I didn't feel like it.

Then he sighed a frustrated sigh (if sighs have emotions) and said if I were really sick why didn't I get into the bed instead of just lying on it?

He went on to the dinner and after a bit I went down and started on some chores. Got going on the fruitcake, chopping the fruits for soaking. Wondering, the while, why I feel compelled to make this fruitcake (which I am certainly nuttier than). J. doesn't much like it, Ames won't eat it on account of her diet, and David never notices what he eats so long as it's sweet. So what's with this fruitcake? I suppose the simple answer is that it is, in my mind anyway, a family tradition and since I am not adhering to the family inwardly I feel I must do so in outward observance.

Sat. was trips to the toilet and housecleaning. Mrs. K. has been somewhat slipshod of late, for which I can't blame her. I am never here to encourage her or to act as if what she does matters and so she feels it doesn't. Got the fruitcake made. Took a big swig of paregoric then rushed to the store to get a poinsettia and some necessities.

J. home early in the afternoon and wanted to know if I was still too sick to go out. Reminded me it was the Mersons' Open House.

Following the fruitcake reasoning, I decided I ought

to go. Figured if I had to spend most of my time in the Mersons' john I would, anyway, be ahead of the game since I don't like Open Houses any more than I do buffet dinners or cocktail parties.

It was the usual Cambridge Collage, bright wool and gray flannel, flowers, ice in glasses, words like NSF, ICBM, MIRV, GAB, IMF, GNP, NIH and names like Henry, Daniel, Arthur, Lee, George floating around . . . all held together with the glue of food and drink. In this case the very best glue because the Mersons have real money (she was a Guggenheim or maybe it was a Rothschild?) and not this worthless Confederate-type paper most of us try to live on.

Everybody *looked* nice; most of them *are* nice and at least 75% of them are right-thinking, well-meaning people so why do these gatherings affect me so adversely?

Once, long ago, I spoke of this to AB who said I was looking for something that wasn't there, for something that I lack in my own life. But now I do not lack for closeness or communication since I have it with Gabriel. Still, I look at the people at these large parties as if they were beings from another planet and I wonder what they are thinking, what motivates them, and what they are getting out of it.

AB asked me what exactly I did not like and while I can say a number of small things, I don't know what the real reason is. I do not like the phony kissing. We all always kiss each other on the cheek (that is, if we're friends of long standing and haven't seen each other since day before yesterday). But that is certainly not the reason for my aversion. And I don't like the necessity for being bright and gay. AB said it was *I* who made that a necessity; that I did not have to be bright and gay. So I suppose that is my own fault and, in any case, that isn't the real reason either.

Maybe it is this feeling that we are all sort of out to display to each other that we are out, that we've been invited to where the action is.

But what action? I mean, what is the action besides just being at this party?

Today (Sun.) David came home and Ames stopped in and I asked her to come to dinner and, wonder of wonders, she said she would. So I rustled around and made lasagna which is one of her favorite dishes and caramel cake which is David's and we had a very pleasant dinner.

J. put himself out to be agreeable, never once calling Ames Meg and not ribbing David the way he sometimes does and I laughed at everything that was remotely funny, and did not pry.

We talked about conservation and pollution. Both Ames and David being concerned that the earth and the fullness thereof will not last out their lives. My deepest conviction is that our exterior pollution is not nearly so threatening as our interior pollution. We are rotten clean through and it seems to me the real question is (to borrow from Faulkner) not whether mankind will just survive but whether it will endure.

While Ames cleared the table and I got the dessert ready, David and J. went out to the yard to find some loose bricks, bricks being what we have to put in the toilet tanks to cut down on water usage. They found some and put them in the toilets which, I am glad to say, seem to flush just as well as before.

After dinner everybody went their separate ways.

Ames back to the Steins, David out with some old pals and J. to his study to work on the eternal backlog.

I did some Xmas stuff, started some laundry and had a long talk with Deb who called to tell me why she had not called before. The reason is that she has been sleeping with a married man (whom I do not know Thank God) and she had not decided what to do about it. She still has not decided but now she wants my advice: should she or should she not go on with this, feeling as she does about women who break up marriages (as she feels Molly broke up hers)?

I hadn't, of course, the faintest idea what she should do so I tried to find out what she wanted to do. It wasn't difficult: she wants to keep on sleeping with the man but with a clear conscience. Which I tried to give her by telling her that marriages are not broken up from the outside but from the inside and the man would not be sleeping with her if there had not been something very wrong at home in the first place.

Which is, I think, true as far as it goes. And it is good enough advice for the moment because Deb hasn't gone very far. What will happen (I think, knowing Deb) is that Deb will begin to feel that if he *really* cares about *her* he can't continue with his wife. But let us not cross that bridge until Deb comes to it.

Afterwards of course I thought of what I had said in relation to myself. And it *is* true that I would never have gotten involved with Gabriel if there were not something wrong with this marriage. But the thought comes unavoidably to mind that there would be a great deal more incentive to try to find a solution within the marriage if one were not getting so much satisfaction outside it. This is not a thought I like to entertain but it has got its foot in the door and I cannot deny its validity. If I had nothing outside this marriage would I not have pressed harder for some solution for us . . . and maybe gotten it??

I could not ever have with J. anything like what I have with Gabriel, that is just not in the cards. But there are other things and one can learn to accommodate oneself to a surprising degree. Viz: Leonard Woolf with Va. I am reading now one of the earlier vols. of his autobiog. and when one sees how extraordinarily difficult it must have been to live with and take care of that poor troubled woman, one wonders what he got out of it. The answer, implicit in his writing, is that what he got was so rewarding that he never even asked himself that question.

And, in another way, so one could wonder about Carrington with Lytton. She knew, she had to know, that he didn't care about her as a woman and that much of the time his heart was with some man. But what she had was more than sufficient. It was enough to bind her to him with hoops of steel.

I think it is a matter of commitment but what I mean by *that* is so involved that I think I will just back off from it and leave it that for now I am committed to Gabriel.

Monday, Dec. 22

Black Monday. A day I will never forget.

I was at Gabriel's early and typing his stuff (he had left a note saying he would be with Rosenblum all morning) when Sam came in.

He refused a cup of coffee and suddenly and without preamble he asked me why I don't let Gabriel leave.

I stared at him, I suppose with my mouth open. And Sam went on. That stuff you're doing (he said) isn't his thesis. That's been approved and there's nothing but technicalities left. Rosenblum's after him to stay here and Gabe would tell him no right off only for you. He can't take you any place south, you know.

Take me south? I said stupidly.

It's nice you so color-blind, Sam said acidly. But you not only white, baby, you wasp-white. You and Gabe wouldn't last long south of the Mason-Dixon.

Are you crazy? I said, feeling that one of us must be. I wouldn't go south with Gabriel. I wouldn't go anywhere with him.

How come? Sam looked at me as if he were measuring me for something, a shroud or a noose, anyway something not nice.

Because I'm an old married woman, that's why. We don't belong together and that's all there is to it. But he didn't tell me. I didn't know.

Well, it's done, Sam said. Now he's got to decide what to do. Didn't you ever think he might be just hanging around here on account of you?

I shook my head.

Sam said that was what Gabriel was doing and if I wanted Gabriel to go I'd have to tell him. I think it's a lot of shit (he said) this going back to teach the tar babies, but that's what Gabe wants . . . he's always wanted that . . . and he ought to have it. Only fly in the ointment is you, baby.

I can't believe it, I said (or I think I said. I was so stunned I didn't know what I was saying). He can't think we could live together. I mean, look at how old I am and all the rest.

It don't matter a damn if you're a hundred, Sam said. What matters is you're white.

The age matters to me, I said. And I've got children and I wouldn't leave them.

All that's your problem, Sam said. I'm telling you the outside problem, the big one you can't get around no way. You're white and you can't go south with Gabe. That's all.

OK, I said. You've told me and I thank you.

No thanks needed, he said. I wasn't doing it for you. Well, what're you going to do about it?

I said I didn't know; that I'd have to think.

Then I put on my coat and said I had to be going. I didn't actually have to go anyplace but I didn't want to see Gabriel until I had really understood and accepted what Sam said.

I drove over to the Cemetery and sat there in the car for a while but somehow it was not a good place to be so I went on out to the Blind School. I was way too early. The party wasn't until the afternoon, but I helped get things ready and then there was the party and afterwards cleaning up.

Home and J. ate a hasty dinner and hurried out to a meeting. I've had all evening to think but I don't seem able to. My mind seems frozen and I feel battered and depleted.

Tuesday, Dec. 23

This morning to the Center briefly. Gabriel in and we had lunch together. I know I have to say something but I don't know what to say. And I don't want to say it. Once I say something, anything, about his leaving the world will come creeping into our lives and it will all be over, even if he has not actually left.

We made a date for tomorrow morning and I will try to say something then.

Wednesday, Dec. 24

Spent a couple of hours this morning at the room with Gabriel. Mostly in bed, drinking coffee, eating sweet rolls and playing records (how will I ever stand to hear "Sitting at the Dock of the Bay" again?).

I tried to say something but I couldn't. He said I seemed down in the dumps and what was the matter? I said it was Xmas, that it always makes me sad. Which is the truth but only a little piece of it.

He is going to Vern's for Xmas but will be back Sat. I have to tell him then.

Friday, Dec. 26

Xmas was all right. It always makes me nostalgic for I don't know what and I am usually awash with emotion. As I was on this one except I was less haunted by the Ghosts of Xmases Past than with thoughts of Gabriel.

Ames came for a middle-of-the-day dinner which was not replete with that old cornball gemutlichness which I am always yearning for. But at least no hostilities broke out. She seemed to like her presents but it is hard to tell what goes on behind that Iron Curtain. Afterwards she went back to the Steins and David (who was clearly delighted with his skis) went up to pack. He was going to Aspen again with Minot, the roommate, (and family) and later I drove him to the airport.

J. and I had invitations to two parties; stopped in at one of them where I felt so much the Spectre at the Feast that I told J. to go on alone to the second party and drop me at home.

He offered to take me to a movie instead which was kind of him since he doesn't like most movies and we bought a paper and found two possibles but there were long lines in front of each so we went on home.

I had been cold all day and by the time we got home I was shivering. I couldn't seem to get warm and I turned on the oven. I was standing practically *in* the oven, with one foot on the open door when J. came in and asked if I were cold. I said I was.

He said it was not, in fact, cold. Then he said, You must be sick.

I waited to see whether he would say I ought to go to bed or I ought to see the doctor.

This time it was both. You ought to go to bed, he said. And if you don't feel better tomorrow you ought to see the doctor.

I said I would but of course I am not sick. Or maybe I am. But not with anything a doctor could help.

Saturday, Dec. 27

J. left for London today.

He was upstairs packing and I brought him up some clean socks and then I sat on the bed watching him, feeling relieved that he was going and feeling bad that I was relieved. He looked to me somehow both vulnerable and brave. Maybe because I know (and he does not) that he is being sinned against. There *is* something brave, almost heroic about him. In the face of my carping disapproval, he remains steadfast and, when I permit (which is not often), cheerful as he goes about trying to plug up the holes in the dikes of the disintegrating world.

Sitting there looking at him I felt great pity. He should've married three other people. Almost any three. Someone who would accept him for what he is (which is, I do know, a considerable person) and not try to wrench him into the demented dream of a soul mate.

I must've looked as low as I felt because J. said, with some surprise, that he'd have thought I'd be glad to see him go; that I acted as if contact with him would defile me.

I said it was the other way around; contact with me would defile him.

He looked at me and asked me what I thought was wrong with me.

I said desperately and off the top of my head that I had B.D.

What's that? he said.

Brain Damage, I said.

And he said coldly, You're not funny.

I hadn't meant to be; it was only just a way of turning the whole thing off. Because it bothers me, it bothers me very much, my life with Gabriel and my non-life with J. And I wished, sitting there looking at The Man in all his Nobility, that he had somebody for himself. Not someone to love. I do not wish that and not (I think) because I am a dog-in-the-manger but because J. is still somehow the rock of my life. But I do wish for him to have someone, someone warm and friendly, to go to bed with.

And thinking of this, I said, You should take advantage of your opportunities. I read in Playboy and Esquire that men like you, men in the prime, who travel around all the time . . . you guys have the pick of all these gorgeous girls at meetings and conferences, secretaries, translators and all.

I suppose you wouldn't mind, he said acidly.

I'd hope I wouldn't have to know, I said.

You don't want an excuse for a divorce? he asked.

I said I didn't want a divorce.

And then . . . and this is awful . . . he sat beside me and tried to sort of ease me back on the bed and pull my skirt up and my panic was so great that I had the strength of ten and I pushed him away and scrambled up. He looked terrible sitting there, depressed, despised and demoralized.

I felt pretty demoralized myself. And depressed. And guilty. To have had interc. with him right then and there would have been an act of simple kindness. And I know it. Why then could I not just let it happen? Why did I feel it would be wrong, sinfully wrong?

I felt terrible and I wanted to make amends but all I could say was, I'm sorry. And then in an embarrassed rush, I added, I do have this B.D.

Oh my God, he said, and he sounded as if he might be laughing or crying and I didn't wait to see but got right out of the room.

Later when I went to the airport with him, he was all crisp and businesslike, giving me his itinerary and reminding me of appointments I have to cancel for him.

When we said goodbye (an exchange of pecks at the air), he said, Take care of that B.D. And somehow that made me feel more kindly to him than I have in a long time.

Still and all, my thoughts went at once to Gabriel and I drove straight there from the airport. I dashed up the stairs expecting to see the door open and Gabriel there but the door was shut and when I went in there was no Gabriel, only a note on the table.

It said: Dearest Girl: I came back but couldn't get you on the phone and I feel too low to sit around. Have gone back to Vern's and am keeping a sleeping bag warm for you. Please come. Here's a map in case you forget the way. xxxxxx G.

I stood there feeling the loneliness and the despair of the long-distance runner who makes it to the end only to find out the race was canceled.

I carefully put his note in my wallet for preserving and left him a note saying to call me as soon as he came in.

The little tree was standing undecorated in the corner; mute evidence (as the novelists say) of Gabriel's state of mind. My own was pretty black as I went home.

It never for a minute occurred to me that I might go to Vern's. I knew, without thinking about it, that I couldn't. It was all right that first time, but it would not be right this time.

I wish there were some way of reaching him but there isn't any phone and a telegram would just never be delivered.

Somehow now I have girded myself for it, I feel a great urgency to tell him he must go south. I worry that he may do something definite about staying here, but the greater worry comes from the feeling . . . conviction really . . . that our time is up and he must go at once (or anyway make plans to go) or something dreadful will happen to us. I will turn into a Pillar of Salt and he will turn into a Pillar of Fire or vice versa. Either way, we will be destroyed.

Called Cissy tonight. Had tried to reach her Xmas Day but nobody answered. She was in and talked, raved in fact, about an encounter group which she and Alex had just returned from.

It blew my mind, she said. I never cried or laughed so much in my life. You and J. should try it. It'll do wonders for your marriage. Or maybe not, one of the couples left on the verge of divorce. But if you've got anything at all to build on, it's beautiful, simply beautiful.

She went on in that vein for a while and when I finally got a word in edgewise I asked about Little Soph. What had happened to her?

Cissy said Soph had gone to Canada with a group of nuts to build some kind of Brook Farm.

I asked about the drug bit and Cissy said, I don't know. And I can't worry about it anymore. One reason we went to the group was to get away from all that. We're *people,* Sophie, not just parents. We all have to remember that we're people.

I asked a few questions about the group, what they were like and so on, and then I asked how she had got Alex to go.

It was his idea, she said. She said he'd given up on the Church. She'd known that wouldn't last and had waited for the next bombshell.

Never dreaming (she said) that he'd come up with this which has been so beautiful for us both.

She certainly did sound happy but I had the feeling that the encounter group will only be a temporary palliative. Still, I suppose that's what life is: a collection of temporary palliatives.

Oh God, I feel awful.

Monday, Dec. 29

Gabriel back today. Came into the Center where I was and at quitting time we went home and I told him.

I started off by saying very casually that it looked to me as if his thesis was almost done and wasn't it time to line up that black university?

He said he wasn't so sure he'd go south right now, and there's a lot of time, and junk like that.

But I kept at it and finally he said he'd been thinking

it over and he thinks it would give him more prestige to teach here for a while, even as a section man, and after a year or two he could get something really good in a black school.

I told him in a year or two he might not want a black school. I told him he didn't need any more prestige, that he needed to have his head examined.

He kidded around a little, calling me Sophie the Slave Driver, trying to get away from the subject.

But I reminded him of all he'd said about being seduced by the big white schools and about how the hope of the great majority of blacks is, and will be for some time, the black schools (or the mainly black schools). You were right then (I said) and you are wrong now.

Sophie-baby, he said, I got a mind of my own and I can change it. After all, Fisk will still be there.

Fisk! I said. Do *they* want you??

Oh, well . . . he said, trying to pass it off. He clearly had not meant to tell me and it had just slipped out. They only said (he said) they might have something.

Might have! I said, jumping at the truth. They have!

And I stared at him appalled. To turn down Fisk which is a good univ. by any standards, Fisk which was (he used to say) more than he could hope for. And I said, Gabriel, if you have turned that down I will kill you. Or anyway I will never see you again.

But if I took the Fisk, I wouldn't see you anyway. So you don't scare me that way (he was still smiling and half-laughing and I could see he was not taking anything I said seriously).

Gabriel, listen to me (I sat across from him at the table and tried to make him be serious). You wouldn't stay here if it weren't for me, isn't that right?

Your little head is getting all swollen up, he said, still smiling. You just part of the picture, not all of it.

I am not any part of the picture, I said. There's no use your staying for any picture that includes me because I will not be in it. (He started to say something but I could see I was getting to him and I went right on.) Gabriel, I lied to you about my age. I am 39 and I will be 40.

You think I care about age? Go on and be 50. You'll still be my Sophie-girl.

I won't look like anybody's Sophie-Girl at 50. Think of me with stiff gray hair, varicose veins on my legs, a roll of fat around my middle, bags under my eyes.

Shut up, he said, pushing his chair back and getting up. Just shut up.

And I could see I had hurt him some way. (Funny how men don't like to hear about the ravages of time, even the ravages on somebody else. J. is the same; when I speak of the ugly footprints of Father Time, he always acts as if I had talked dirty. Maybe they are more afraid of the idea of mortality than we are?)

OK, I said. But it would be hard enough for us being black and white. When people begin helping me across the street while they're asking you to go out on pot parties . . . well, you would die of shame and I would have to put my head in the oven.

How long you plan to keep this up? He said it as coldly as he's ever said anything to me.

Until you see it's hopeless, I said. Because there is no future for us, not only in the south, but not here either. Not anywhere.

Then he tried to make me come sit on the bed beside him but I wouldn't. He said something about how some things are more important than others and a lot of in-volved stuff about what he could do here that he couldn't do at Fisk. And finally, he said, Sophie, I do not want to leave you.

We will not see each other if you stay so you might as well go, I said.

And never see you again?

Oh, never is a long time (I thought how young he is). We'll see each other sometime.

But not like this, he said.

I agreed it would not be like this. But by that time, whenever that will be, you'll have somebody else, I said.

He shook his head and said no.

And I thought again how young he is. And I thought too of how he would most certainly have someone else, maybe a lot of someones. I am the one who will never have anyone else. Never anyone again. But all I said was, Want to bet fifty cents?

He reached into his pocket and he held out his hand with two quarters in it. I folded his fingers over and kissed them and told him I would not take money from a blind man. Then I got up and said I had to get on home.

He put his arms around me and held me and I stood there thinking that this was harder than it had any right to be. And then I thought maybe I would just cop out, hop a plane tomorrow for Cissy's and send him a letter from there.

And just then, Gabriel said against my ear, I got a funny feeling you might not come back. You wouldn't pull everything down and just walk away, would you?

And then I knew that of course I couldn't do that. And I said I wouldn't. But I will make a pact with you, I said. We will go on just as before and for as long as we can, if you will take the Fisk offer.

He moved back and looked at me with his large beautiful eyes. Suppose I refuse? he said.

You got no choice, I said. It's that or nothing. (And I felt about 99 yrs. old as I said it and as ugly as the picture of Dorian Gray.)

I've got to think, he said. I'll see you tomorrow?

I said he would and he kissed me on the forehead and he said, You are one mean, hateful child, Sophie.

I drove home thinking I had done pretty well and that very likely he would agree to go. But after I let myself in, I felt I had done a terrible thing and I hoped to God he wouldn't go. The house was quiet and empty, almost spooky, Ames at the Steins, David in Aspen, J. in London . . . and me here in Purgatory.

I walked around turning on all the lights, including the Xmas tree ones, but that did not make me feel any better so I turned them all off and came upstairs.

How I wish I had, as we used to laughingly say when I was young, a mother to guide me. Not really to guide me, but to bolster me up and remind me that this has to be done. Somebody who would say, You're doing right, Sophie. Stick with it.

Tuesday, Dec. 30

It is now seven in the a.m. and I am sitting here in the kitchen with the oven and the lights on (the house hasn't warmed up and it's still dark out) hoping to get this down while it is still clear in my head.

Last night (after I had written about Gabriel) I went to bed but I couldn't sleep so I finally came down and I was here in the kitchen making some Sanka when I heard a noise at the front door.

Sure that it was the doom I hourly expect I grabbed a knife from the rack and hotfooted it out to the front hall. It was Ames letting herself in with her key. She was wearing her party Dashiki and she would've looked very pretty except her face was odd-looking.

She didn't say anything as she went into the living room, just threw her coat on a chair and scrunched herself down into a corner of the sofa. I followed (concealing the evidence of my cowardice under a newspaper on the table) and trying to be ever so casual, I asked her what was wrong.

Everything's wrong, she said. I'm wrong and I don't know what's right. And then she started to cry.

Instantly the internal Old Faithful started gushing a fountain of sympathy and protectiveness but I knew I mustn't let it out or it would drown us both so I said I'd be right back and I went out and made some hot Nesquik which used to be her favorite drink.

When I came back with it she had unscrunched herself and was blowing her nose. She said, Thanks, Mom, and drank some and I felt this great warmth and I realized it was because this was the first thing I had been able to do for her in so long I can't remember. Must everybody feel needed? Or is it just women? Or just me?

She looked around the room and she looked at her cup and she drank some more and finally she said, Hey, Mom, what age do I have to start taking the pill?

I had thought of all kinds of things she might say,

like "I've got syphilis" or "I am the leader of a teen-age gang of thieves." But if my life depended upon it, I wouldn't have guessed she'd say what she did. So I asked her why she asked.

She hemmed and hawed with all those "Well's" and "You know's" that they use but finally she launched into it.

There had been a dance at school and she and Gretchie and some others had gone together. She was "sort of" with Jackie. She asked if I remembered him and I nodded, not saying that the minute I heard his name an early warning system went off in my head and I thought, Aha! The Jewel Thief!

From time to time some of the kids went out to the parking place where there was pot and liquor. Jackie went and kept trying to get her to go. She refused at first but finally she did go.

I didn't want to, she said, but somehow he always makes me feel like guilty when I don't do what he wants.

When I heard the word "guilty" a whole battery of burglar alarms went off and I could almost have guessed the rest. Almost but not quite.

They went to a car where he had a bottle and he had a few drinks, but she didn't and she kept making noises about going back and he kept making motions about . . .

Making out, she said. He didn't actually say so and at first I thought I must be imagining things, like I had a dirty mind, you know. But when he began yanking at the neck of my dress and trying to, you know, get up the bottom, I figured it was for real and I told him no. So he said, What's the matter? Forget your pill?

(At this my stomach became a hard little ball and I

wanted to throw something but I sat there as quietly as old Ass Bird dozing in his chair, keeping my eyes down and my breathing even.)

She told him she was not on the pill. He said that was OK; that he had some Saran Wrap.

(Here my eyes flew open and bugged out but I carefully kept my mouth shut.)

She told him he was a great guy and she liked him a lot but she didn't feel like it, all the while trying to fend off the grappling hooks.

Then he asked her what she was saving it for? a white prick? (she said the words clearly but her face was a brick-red). Then she slapped him and got out. She told Gretchie she didn't feel well and one of the chaperones brought her home.

I didn't tell Gretchie, she said. I didn't want to rat on him but I guess it's OK to tell you because, well, you're like safe and I have to tell somebody. Because I feel so bad, so guilty, see? Because he's black and I think *he* thinks it was because of that. But it wasn't anything to do with that. Honest it wasn't. I'm just well like not ready. Maybe I'm retarded but I don't want to now. Not yet. Not with anybody.

And all the while I was raging inside. If he had been within striking distance I think I would've struck him.

You did exactly the right thing, I told her. And there's no reason for you to feel guilty. He's a real 24-karat bastard to try to blackmail you into doing what he wanted.

It *was* kind of like blackmail, wasn't it? she said looking relieved. Then suddenly she said, Oh jeez, we shouldn't have used that word.

I looked blank and she explained. Blackmail, she

said. We learned about that and lots of other words in the Seminar. Blackmail, blackball, black heart, they're all racist words.

But my God! I said. Blackmail has nothing to do with blacks. It's an old, old word from Scotland where some chiefs used to demand tribute or they'd ransack the villages, kind of like the Mafia. You can't drop every word with black in it out of the language.

No, she said. But the words with bad connotations, those should go.

My God! I said again. There are lots of words that have color in them that simply have nothing to do with blacks. Take the black flag, for one; that's the flag of a pirate. Would that be considered racist? And then there's the white flag and that's a synonym for cowardice. Is that racist? I mean, how can I talk if I can't call a spade a spade and say the future looks black?

Ames laughed and said we could use blackmail and she did think that's what it was. But he does always have it on his mind, she said. His color, I mean. And like with those words, I guess some blacks do think everything's on account of color.

But you know this wasn't, I said. If you lived in the south and you and Jackie were out together and somebody insulted him, or you, you could be pretty sure it was racism. And here and now, if you had slept with him it would also have been racism, a reverse racism, but racism just the same. You would've treated him differently from the way you'd have treated an ordinary white boy.

But he isn't an ordinary white boy. He's black and color does count. You've got to admit it counts.

Everything counts, I said. Skin color, age, sex, accent, manners and education. Black is beautiful and blondes have more fun. The point is, honey, what importance these things have for *you.*

She looked kind of dubious and I said, Look at it this way. Suppose you knew he wanted to sleep with you just because you're white. How would you like that?

I wouldn't, she said.

I asked her why not and she said, Well, because it would mean I wasn't important. I mean, me, myself. It would be like he wanted something about me that isn't important and I'd feel kind of, well, you know, downgraded.

I told her she had said it all right there. It's the human being that's important (I said) and you stick to that. Never mind Strom Thurmond or Jackie. Some old Greek said we must take the best of human doctrines and embark on that as the raft on which to risk the voyage of life. I think it was Plato but it might've been Socrates. Anyway, it was somebody reliable. And you've got yourself a good raft. Hang onto it.

Then I asked her if she was hungry and she said she was so we went out to the kitchen.

While I heated the milk and she made the toast she said how hard it was for her to keep from acting the way other people wanted her to act.

Sometimes (she said) I feel like I don't have any real identity at all. I mean, like one day I'm one person and the next day I'm somebody else. Do you think I'm having like an identity crisis?

I asked what she thought. And she said she thought she was not. But lots of kids my age do have them, she said. I guess I'm kind of retarded there too. Still, I suppose you could say it gives me something to look forward to.

And she gave a funny grin that warmed me all over.

She munched on the toast and as I wiped up the milk I had spilled I looked at her bare calloused feet resting on the open oven door and I thought of how these kids remind me of Our Boys at Valley Forge with their beat-up boots (the uppers on Ames's have left the soles in places), their bare legs in arctic weather, their worn jeans and old army jackets. Their sufferings and deprivations, sometimes gratuitous (but not always: Ames gave 3 months' allowance to some draft-card burner's defense) seem to me to be Patents of Nobility (or do I mean Portents? Maybe both).

Then suddenly Ames said, Hey, Mom, what *about* the pill? Do people just automatically start on it when they get their driver's permits or what?

I hesitated, trying to think exactly what to say. I've given a lot of thought to what I think about the pill and kids and, specifically, what I think about sex and my single girl. And I was about to take off on what could've been the world's longest (and dullest) lecture on sex-morals-and-biology when I remembered, just in time, that good old Spock advice about telling kids only what they asked.

So I said there weren't any rules about it and here again it was for her to decide what was right for her. I said there were some indications that it might not be good to take the pill for long periods. And I told her some of what I had heard at the lecture on contraception.

It doesn't (I said) seem like good sense to start it for no reason. To take it now with nothing in mind is putting the cart before the horse.

She laughed and said, You mean like get the horse first?

I said yes but please not a horse's ass like Jackie.

How'd you like that Saran Wrap? she said still laughing.

I said the boy was a public menace. That stuff tears and breaks, I said, and some of it even has holes in it.

We talked a little longer and she swore me to secrecy; said I must never tell her father about it; that he might cut out after Jackie with a shotgun. He's pretty old-fashioned, you know, she said.

Then as we staggered up the stairs she said she was glad I'd been home. I could've doped it out myself (she said) but it was nice to have somebody to talk to.

She went to her room and I went to mine and got into bed and lay propped up with my book not seeing a word of it, trying to make my insides stop shaking. Because I was, almost literally, all shook up. I had looked calm (I hope) but I had not been calm and now it was over I felt as if I had just got off a very thin, very high wire. I hope what I said was right. I think I said what I believe to be right.

All the time she was talking the irony of it struck me . . . it could not, of course, help but strike me . . . Ames with her bad black boy and me with my good one.

Gabriel is everything any mother would want for her daughter: kind, intelligent, thoughtful, gentle and tough when it is necessary to be tough. Jackie, on the other hand, is (at least right now) a wholly repulsive clod; very like some fraternity men I remember who had little on their minds beyond drinking and screwing and who became very nasty when you didn't put out for them.

When I think of what Ames has ahead of her with this business of putting out or not putting out! People like Jackie undoubtedly think they're behaving perfectly normally and, for this society, they probably are.

I do hope and pray Ames will grow to be strong enough to do what she wants to do for her own good reasons. She seems to be shaping up that way . . . she came through this with flags flying. I love that girl so much. And seeing her good sense tonight, I am at last ready to let her go. Greater love hath no mother.

Still Tuesday, Dec. 30

Gabriel says he will take the Fisk.

We spent the day together, starting at about ten when I went over and waked him. He said he hadn't decided anything and there was no hurry and I could see he intended to stall as long as he could. So I kept after him all day, at breakfast at the Waldorf, at the Fogg where we went to walk around and look in on his Mam, at lunch back at the room, in bed in the afternoon and later while we were ice skating.

I did, I thought then, a pretty neat job. I was agreeable and friendly (even loving) but I did not allow him to slip away from the arguments which were, for the most part, all ones *he* had given *me* last fall as to why it is so important to go back and the great danger of staying here (or any place like here). He had nothing to answer except about losing me but I had already answered that and I didn't relax a jot on it. But still he would not say he would go.

We were having dinner at the cheap fish place when

I said something I had been thinking about in the back of my mind, something which did not seem to be of much importance but I said it anyway.

There is one thing (I said) that we haven't mentioned at all in this. And that is how I'd feel if you went back on your high resolve.

Oh, Christ, that high resolve! he said. Why did I ever open my big watermelon mouth?

Never mind that, I said. You did and you convinced me, beyond any doubt, that what you wanted then is right. How would I feel if I knew that I had had a part in changing you, in making you less than you were?

Oh, Sophie, Sophie! he said. Why does it have to be less? There's plenty I can do here, *plenty*.

It's not the same. You know it isn't, I know it isn't. And you'd have given up the best part of you for nothing because we wouldn't see each other. And here we'd be, you doing your paltry little thing here and me sitting in my big fat house eating pieces of my heart every day because I'd know it was at least partly my fault. Isn't that a pretty crummy thing to do to me?

He picked at his fish and he did not look happy as he said, But if I were doing what I *wanted* to do . . .

It ain't permitted, I said. After the Prophet has read off the Tablets and shown the way to the Promised Land he can't lie down and say "You go on without me, boys, I think I'll rest here a little."

He grinned and said he had no Tablets and no map.

I said he didn't need a map to know which way to go. You are (I told him) a prophet, and if you're going to turn your back on your teachings I will put on a hair shirt and hire a Harvard boy to throw ashes on me.

Why does what *I* do have to make so much difference? he protested.

Because it does, I said. And then, suddenly I felt as all gone as a deflated balloon. It seemed to me that not only was it hopeless but it was hopeless because of me and I said I couldn't say anything more.

We had eaten all we were going to eat so we left and drove back to the room and he said would I come up and I said no, that he had to think by himself.

He said, All right. Then he kissed my cheek and he said, You are a flint-stone, Sophie.

I said there was nobody at home but me now and would he call me if he had anything to say. He said he would. Then he said, But I'll see you tomorrow anyway?

I said I supposed so. I wasn't trying to blackmail (Oh, that word!) him but I was so tired I was almost physically sick and I couldn't muster any emotion but weariness.

I went home and it was along about ten when the phone rang. It was Gabriel. He said, Sophie? I decided you wouldn't look so good in a hair shirt so I'll go.

I gulped and then without thinking at all I said, I love you very much. And I hung up. And I cried. Of course I cried.

Wednesday, Dec. 31

Today to the Center. Gabriel came and got me at lunchtime. We seem to have decided to be cheerful and matter-of-fact about his going, at least that is what we were. He said he had tried to see Rosenblum this morning but R. wasn't in. He had tracked him down at home and would go there this afternoon.

But, Sophie-girl, he said, you needn't think you're getting rid of me right off. I don't know *when* they want somebody out there. For all I know it might be next year.

I said that was fine; just so long as things were moving.

Then suddenly (I guess he remembered my saying I was home alone) he said, Hey! You can come to the party tonight! And he explained there is to be a New Year's Eve party, Sam and a bunch of his Brandeis friends and some other kids, at somebody's apartment near Inman Square. He had planned to go because he'd thought I'd have to be home. But now, he said, we can both go.

I said how sorry I was but I couldn't. Ames was having some friends in and I had to be there to kind of help and oversee (I wonder if *that's* a bad word) the proceedings.

He looked disappointed (but not dejected) and said, Well, but what about New Year's Day?

And I said fine and we'd spend it together.

Of course Ames is not having friends in but I wouldn't dream of going to any kids' party with Gabriel. I've been to student parties with J. and I always feel we have both grown long white beards before the evening is over. Partly, with J., it is because he is a professor and profs (and their wives) come with long white beards as standard equipment. But even so, it would never in this world do for me to go to a kids' party with Gabriel.

I went home and I was crawling around under the Xmas tree, putting water in its little cup (how I do try to prolong that tree every damn year) when I heard the door open and great shouts of merriment.

It was Ames and Gretchie. They were moving in. Said they were sick of the Steins'; said there were too many old kids (Gretchie's brothers and sisters) in and out and creating (they said) such a stink with their cigarettes and booze that the place was positively cancerous.

We came over here, Ames said, to get a little fresh air.

Don't you ever drink? Gretchie asked me.

And Ames said hardly at all and that I never got silly the way "most of them do." Which made me feel as if I had been awarded the Legion d'Honneur.

Postcard from J. today. Picture of the Changing of the Guard at Buckingham Palace. The card said, Remember when we first saw this? Love, J.

That surprised me some. I certainly do remember. Ames was not yet two and J. held her on his shoulders. It was the summer we rented a car and drove around England and Scotland. It was one of our happiest times and it seems only about as long ago as the time of the Cave Paintings. I wonder at his remembering it. He never remembers anything like that. His p. cards usually say "It rained today. Love, J." or "My plane was late. Love, J."

Perhaps he did find that gorgeous secretary and has been shaken up some? Or maybe there IS a heart under all that GNP?

Ames and Gretchie fussed around the rest of the afternoon. What should they do to celebrate New Year's? They didn't want to go to somebody's big binge and they didn't want to sit home and didn't want to ask anybody over and what should they do.

As we were eating dinner the big idea came to them. They would take the car (Gretchie has her license) and go to a drive-in for a midnight movie, and what did I think of that? Wasn't it the most?

So after dinner, I gave them the keys to my little car (little cars have less pollution and more status, they told me) and they set off for the nearest heater-in-your-car drive-in. I asked them what was playing and they laughed hysterically and said, Who cares? The thing is to GO.

That seems to be the text with which we start the New Year: the thing is to go.

I am reading another Shackleton book (this is his own story of that incredible time) and that seems to be his message also. When he sets out in the *James Caird*, he knows their chances of survival are slim but to stay is certain death so the thing is to go.

That is true for Gabriel and, I expect, in some kind of way true for me too. Not that my "going" need be physical . . . but I will have to leave where I've been and strike out for something else.

Jan. 1, 1970

Left the girls sleeping and went about nine to Gabriel's. He was up and dressed in heavy clothes and was packing bread, cheese and other stuff into a plastic bag.

What are we doing? I asked looking at the preparations (there were 4 other filled bags sitting on the floor). Going to cross the Pole?

Just about, he said. We're going back to Ipswich to the beach. Remember we said we'd go?

I took off my coat and started stowing away the stuff. Then I said, You know there are two inches of snow on the ground and, according to the weather report, gusts up to 29 miles an hour. I mean, Boss, it will be COLD.

He said he didn't think it would be all that cold. It's bound (he said) to get warmer.

Or colder, I said.

He laughed and said, Well, are you with me?

I said I was and that I was proud to be associated with a spiritual heir of Shackleton's. Then I asked him when he'd got all this food and he said he'd bought it yesterday afternoon, after he had decided where we'd go today. And it's all done (he said). I've got everything and we can go.

So we took one of his blankets and the bags and put them in the car. I wanted to get warmer clothes so we drove by here and I ran in and got my sheepskin coat and the lined boots and at the last minute I grabbed up Shackleton and the old plaid blanket. The girls were eating breakfast and said Good morning.

They looked at me in my arctic clothes and Ames said, What're you going to do, build igloos?

I said that's just what I was going to do and maybe I wouldn't be home for dinner.

As I went out I heard Gretchie say, You know, your mother's pretty cool, for a parent, that is.

And I laughed to myself at the extraordinary accolade but also at the thought of how really too much she would think it if she knew I was going to Ipswich to build igloos with my child-groom (shows you how little chance the older woman has in this world. Child-bride is common currency in fact and in language but there is no such thing as a child-groom).

Then, just as I was about to get in the car, I thought of a shovel and I ran back to the front door and took the one on the porch.

You think we'll need that? Gabriel said as I shoved it behind the seats.

I said I didn't know but I had learned from Shackleton that you had to be prepared for anything.

Gabriel wanted to know who this Shackleton was. He had never heard of him!

So it was with great pleasure that I told him about that heroic man. His aim (I said) was to cross the polar continent from sea to sea but he never made it. His ship was crushed by ice floes before they ever got there but their long trek from way south of the Antarctic Circle to safety is something to make you stand up and cheer. I've got it with me and if we're not snowed out you can read it today.

We got there and parked as close as we could and then we lugged the stuff over the dunes to the beach. It *was* cold but not as cold as it could've been. I mean, it *felt* as if we would turn into solid blocks of ice but we didn't and pretty soon we got a space cleared and a fire started and then we went up the beach foraging for more wood.

We didn't find much and it was wet but usable when drenched with the fire lighter. Pretty soon we were sitting on the blanket, toasting franks over the fire and drinking lemon-mush (melted frozen lemonade drizzled over ice) through straws (he had thought of everything).

Then we walked some more and it was beautiful. I mean *really* beautiful (not the kind of beautiful Cissy was talking about). The wind was sharp and fresh; the water was black and gray and wild; the beach clean and open and it was as if we were the first people ever on it.

We went back, and leaned against the dunes and watched the fire and it seemed to me it was the most beautiful day in the world. I thought the sun shone but I am not too sure that it actually did.

After a while, with the other blanket over us, we fell asleep. It was somewhat like that time at Vern's sleeping in front of the open fire, only here we were all alone and not separated by sleeping bags.

When we awoke, whatever there had been of sun was gone and the fire was out. And now it was really cold. I thought it was time to go but I didn't say anything because I soon saw that Gabriel didn't want to.

Let's race down the beach, he said. And then come back and build another fire. I've got dinner too.

It touched me terribly that he had planned so much on this day but I had determined not to let one single sad thought cross my mind so I shut it right out and said, On your mark. And I ran until I almost literally dropped. Even in my youth I would never have been any match for that fleet-footed boy (I do believe he has Indian blood) but now in my senescence it is hopeless.

Then we walked even further down the beach, and around a little point we came on a rowboat half on its side, sort of propped up on a stake.

Look! I said. The *James Caird!*

Is that Shackleton's boat? the bright boy said.

One of them, I said. It was the lifeboat he set out in to get help. He and some of the crew sailed in open seas 800 miles in a boat not much bigger than this.

The boat was tilted just enough so one could get

under it and sit there, sheltered from the wind. So we did. And we fell on each other and we slept together there under the protection of the *James Caird.* It was not cold and not even very awkward. I have got adept at pulling things down and lifting things up (which is one reason I always wear a skirt with Gabriel) and the strange thing is that none of this ever seems strange to me. Just perfectly natural and reasonable.

Then we went back and tried to build up the fire but we had very little wood so we couldn't get but a small blaze going. Still, it was cheery and in the gathering dusk we ate salami and cheese and he told me some about last night's party and I told him some about Shackleton.

It got dark and still we sat, holding hands, the blanket wrapped around our legs. And then finally a mist began to fall and I knew I would cry if we sat there any longer so I got up and pulled him up and said, Come on, Boss, the men are waiting for us back at Elephant Island.

And we got going on burying the ashes and packing up the debris, and I got through that touch-and-go moment when I was about to turn into that dreadful creature of which I had had a prevision, Lana Turner crying over the love that-could-not-be.

Going back he seemed so happy that I could not help feeling good myself. We told jokes or rather he did since I never can remember the punch lines.

It was well into the evening when we got back and Gabriel wanted me to come in but I said no I had to get home to the kids. I didn't really but I felt sadness rising in me like a flood tide and I wanted to get off by myself before I was swamped.

I came home to find the girls painting Ames's room. I asked where they had got the paint and they said they had gone around the neighborhood begging any old paint and had dumped it all together. I thought it a hideous color, somewhere between mauve and puce, but I said it was magnificent and left them to it.

Have been up here reading Shackleton and soon to bed. I'm tired enough from all that walking and running to sleep soon (I hope). Shackleton has been an enormous help to me. I cling to what he said after the ship was utterly crushed and he had to plan how to get through. He said (and I have memorized it): A man must shape himself to a new mark directly the old one goes to ground.

I keep telling myself that this is not the end of the world and that I will shape myself to a new mark. I keep telling myself but inside something keeps crying, Oh, don't leave me, don't leave me.

Saturday, Jan. 3

Gabriel is gone. This day he is gone forever. He says not and maybe he even thinks not but it is forever. It really really is.

He broke the news that he was leaving yesterday. And he broke it in such a way I nearly collapsed.

I had gone by the room early (yesterday morning) but he wasn't there so I went on to the Blind School. After the lesson, when I came out, there he was on the steps. I guess I must have mentioned I was going there Friday and he had made his way by subway, bus and foot and had waited for me.

I almost fell down when I saw him. I was afraid something dreadful had happened. But as he drove us home he told me. Yesterday Fisk called Rosenblum and said if Gabriel wants the job, he has to come now. Something about taking over somebody's course in midstream. He'll have to come back if he wants to pick up his degree. He says he will, but I think he will change his mind once he's gone.

Anyway, he was all excited about it (and why wouldn't he be?) and said he had come out to get me because we only had until the next day (today) and he didn't want to waste any time.

I said he was right because one thing we had to do was get him some clothes. He has nothing but jeans and no jackets at all.

He said that *would* be a waste of time and not what he was thinking of at all. And he smiled as he said it.

And for once we were not one person. I smiled because he did but I did not feel like smiling. I didn't feel like going to bed either but I knew he did. I felt like lying down in the street and weeping or just opening the car door and jumping out. But I did not feel like going to bed.

He did agree to get something to put on his back and we went and bought a jacket. He refused to buy the ubiquitous gray flannel trousers, saying if he turned up in those they'd think he was an effete intellectual snob and he'd never win the confidence of the natives. I was glad he didn't get the gray flannels. He is right and my thinking of them was a remnant of my Establishmentarianism.

Then we got some food and went to the room and I knew as we went up the stairs that as soon as we got inside he would want to go to bed. He did and so of course I undressed and got under the covers.

It was going along but I had my eyes shut tight, trying to stay out of it so I would not cry, so I didn't notice anything until I heard this wrenching cry, Sophie! Sophie! and I opened my eyes and saw there were tears on his face.

Afterwards as he lay back on the pillow, he said, I shouldn't have said I'd go. I feel like my arm is being cut off. This is too much, Sophie, too much.

I knew if I hesitated an instant I would be lost. So I got right up, put on Gabriel's robe, grabbed up my clothes and hurried out to the bathroom.

I went to the john and washed my face, taking a long time about it, but still I didn't feel able to go back. So I got into the shower. But, as I pulled the curtain and turned on the water, the thought that this was the last time I would ever be in this shower hit me with such painful force that I turned the water off and got out and dressed. It was odd but somehow, right then, the fact that I would never take another shower in that place grieved me beyond belief.

When I came back Gabriel was dressed and staring into an open footlocker. My God, Sophie! he said, looking horror-struck at me. There's years of work right in this trunk alone. How'll we ever get it all done?

And there was a lot to do. Sorting and throwing out and packing and telephoning Sam and some of the others. And some of them came by and somebody brought some beer and somebody else a bottle and at various points people went out to get food and cardboard cartons.

Sometime in the afternoon Gabriel went out to look for a used suitcase. I was packing books when Sam came over to me and said, You done good, Sophie.

Better than you'd have expected from a white woman, I said.

Yes, he said. Then, You really got a thing for the kid, don't you?

I said No, that I had just been looking for a place to come in out of the rain.

You don't like me much, do you? he said.

You can't (I said) go beating up on a Wasp's Nest and expect the Wasp to like you.

He kind of grinned. Then he stuck out his hand and said, Peace?

I took his hand and said Peace. Then I said maybe when the Revolution came he'd save me from the White Concentration Camps in Mississippi.

Then he really smiled and he said he would put in a good word for me.

Around dinnertime I told Gabriel I had to go home and check on the girls but I'd be back in an hour or two. The girls were in and said they'd be delighted to fix their own supper. I said I probably wouldn't be back. I may stay with Deb tonight, I said (Oh honest Sophie). You can reach me there in case you need me.

That left them laughing, in case they needed me! And I went upstairs and called Deb (feeling ashamed that I haven't had any time for her in weeks). I asked her straight out if I could use her. I said I would give her a number that she was to use only in a real emergency.

My God, Sophie, she said, what are you up to?

I said I was on a secret underground mission and I gave her Gabriel's number and told her to keep ringing and that my code name was Gabriel.

Then I sat trying to think what I could give Gabriel to take with him. Something of my very own, not something bought. I knew it was sentimental, maybe selfish, but I didn't care. It seemed as if it wouldn't hurt so much when he left if something of me could go with him. And then I thought of it . . . the heavy old signet ring of my father's that I had had made smaller so I could wear it. I looked at it on my finger and tried it on my little finger and I was sure it would fit his little finger.

When I went back the others had left and we went on packing and sorting and throwing out. Finally when we were almost done we walked up to the Chinese place and had egg rolls and sweet and sour.

Walking back, he said, You're spending the night, Sophie. He didn't ask it, he said it. And of course I was.

We went back to the room, so tired we could hardly drag ourselves along, only to find there were still cartons to be tied and that the bed was covered with old books and newspapers.

By the time we finally got into the bed, we could barely see to kiss each other goodnight and we fell asleep at once.

Then . . . much later it must have been because the moon was very pale outside the window . . . I awakened and he was sleeping. So I lay there looking up at the piece of sky I could see and I thought of that poem I used to love so much when I was young and romantic.

I couldn't remember all of it but the part I could remember was for this time and this place.

Where like a pillow on a bed, the pregnant back swelled up to rest the violet's reclining head, sat we two, one another's best. Our eyebeams twisted and did thread our eyes upon one double string . . . so to engraft our hands was all the means to make us one . . . and pictures in our eyes to get was all our propagation.

And pictures in our eyes to get was all our propagation.

And then he opened his eyes and said, Sophie? And we put our arms around each other and this time it was like a blessing, like the first time he kissed me.

And then it was morning and Thank the Good Lord it was late so we had no time for anything but hurrying to catch the plane.

He was driving with one hand and holding mine with the other, and I was trying to think how to tell him I wanted him to have this ring when it occurred to me I could just put it on his finger. I did and it was a little tight but it went on.

What? he said, looking at it. What's this?

I told him it was the oldest thing I had and I wanted him to take it and not say anything about it.

Then we were in the tunnel and then out of it and in about one minute we were in front of his airline.

He looked at me and he said, When I am an old old man, I will tell my grandchildren about you. I will say, you want to know who gave me this ring? My girl Sophie gave me this ring.

It's late, I said and I opened the door and got out.

He took his suitcase out of the back and when I said I was not going in with him, he put his arms around me and we held each other until our bones should have broken. And then I pulled away and I ran around the car and got in and drove off as quickly as I could.

I came home but I couldn't stand it here so I went to a movie. I don't know what it was only there was a lot of shooting. I called the girls and told them to fix themselves some supper. I had some coffee but I didn't eat. Every place I went I had been to with Gabriel and I had no appetite.

I went to another movie but it turned out to be an

old Ingmar Bergman I had seen with Gabriel so I left that and came home.

I have washed and waxed the kitchen floor and now I am sitting in the kitchen with the little TV on (just the picture not the sound) and soon I will go to bed and I hope I die before dawn.

Sunday, Jan. 11

J. is back.

I met him at the airport and he seemed not like himself, diffident or something. And as we drove home, I realized he was kind of offering apologies. Not in so many words, but he was saying he had realized this time in London that his life had become a rat race of conferences and meetings and he never has time for his students, let alone his family. He said it was going to be different from now on, that he was cutting down and cutting back.

I suppose he expected me to cry Eureka! but all I could manage was that that would be quite a change.

He reiterated that the way we have been living is impossible and that it is over and life is too short and a lot more in that vein.

I found it dimly touching that he was trying so hard, but only dimly. Nothing has been anything but dim these last days.

Ames and Gretchie were home for dinner which was a help as they talked a lot which covered my silence. After dinner, J. wanted to take me out. Anywhere you want to go, he said.

I tried to think of something to oblige him but there was nowhere I wanted to go.

A movie, he said. There must be something you want to see.

I said I had seen everything. Which is true. I've been to the movies every day for the last week.

Finally I took pity on him and said I had bills to pay and calls to make. So why didn't he go to the Univ. and collect his mail. Which he did. Of course I didn't pay any bills or make any calls. As soon as he left I went at the kitchen floor again. I've washed and waxed it every night and it seems to help more than anything else.

When J. came back I was sitting in front of the TV, watching I don't know what. He sat down and clearly wanted to talk some about the conference so I turned the sound off (*quelle politesse*) and listened. Finally he said he was tired and it was the middle of the night by his body-time and he was going to bed. I said I would stay down awhile and I turned the sound back on.

And I sat there wondering what I was doing and what I was going to do. And . . . most of all . . . what I wanted to do. For that was what I didn't know. I had felt more dead than alive since Gabriel left and I had not wanted anything at all. And I still did not feel I wanted anything.

So I sat and stared dry-eyed at this monster movie (it seemed to be about some Bug People) and I began to feel like a monster myself . . . a cold, soulless monster all alone on a great empty plain.

I hurt so bad inside, right in the middle of me, that it came to me that this is the reason for hara-kiri. If one hurts so much there is only one thing to do and that is to plunge the knife in and cut out that intolerable hurt.

But a middle-aged, middle-class white woman in Cambridge, Mass., cannot commit hara-kiri. It would be unseemly and would cast a cloud over my dearly beloved middle-class children. Besides which I have neither the means nor the wits for such a deed.

And I tried to think what to do. Not, anymore, what I wanted to do but just what there was to do. I thought of Shackleton and his words, a man must shape himself to a new mark directly the old one goes to ground. I thought of the *James Caird* and how Shackleton had set out in it, not knowing what would befall him. I thought of Gabriel setting off in his beautiful black skin for Tennessee not knowing what awaits him.

And I thought of commitment and it came to me that that is what the Gabriels and the Shackletons have. And I realized what had been there all the time: nobody gives you that commitment, you have to dredge it up yourself.

Just then I noticed that the monsters were gone from the TV and there was now a minister (or a priest or a rabbi) who was saying that the thought for the end of this day would be from Ecclesiastes. And I waited for The Word with the same superstitious belief that I scan all signs and portents, including messages in fortune cookies.

And the man said, Whatsoever thy hand findeth to do, do it with thy might for there is no work, nor device, nor knowledge, nor wisdom in the grave whither thou goest.

And it was The Word, all right, the very same word on which I had been brooding. And I knew as surely as I knew my name that despite our two children and our 99 years of marriage, I had never committed myself to J. as

I had to Gabriel; that I had never accepted J. as I had Gabriel, with all my might, all my mind and heart and body.

I got right up, turned off the TV and crept upstairs to our bathroom. I undressed in the dark and, as I threw my clothes over the shower curtain rod, I thought of the shower at Gabriel's. Tears ran out of my eyes. I grabbed up a towel and held it to my face, surprised at the tears and indignant at them too. I had (have) truly given Gabriel up. I did not regret it and I could not wish him back. But still I cried.

My face was in the towel when I heard J. come into the room. Sophie? he said. Are you crying?

I gave a final wipe and said no, that I had just washed my face.

I turned to put the towel back and I saw him looking at me in the dim light coming through the window from the street. I stood there, naked and cold, and I knew I had to try now, right now. That wasn't true, I said to him. I was crying.

I reached out and he put his arms all the way around me and said, Let me help.

My mind went back to the Biblical Word and I said, Comfort me with apples. Then, as I felt the tears coming up again, I said, Or with anything else you have around.

Come to bed, J. said as he moved us into the bedroom. And I'll see what I can find.

We got into bed and he held me. I've missed you, missed you every day for months. It's been a long hard winter. Then, holding me closer, he said, But the winter is past, the rain is over and gone.

Surprised, I said I didn't know he ever read the Bible. He said he was once briefly a Sunday School teacher and I asked why had he never told me. He said he had but that sometimes I didn't listen.

I was going to say that I always listened but I started to wonder if I really did. And then he kissed me and I think at some point he even said my name. I know I heard it and I knew then (and now) that it was all right for me to give and get this comfort.

Afterwards, as I was lying there staring at the ceiling, I said, J., I want another child.

Child? he said. You mean you want to have a baby?

I said no, that there were too many babies in the world; that I wanted to adopt one, a good-sized one that nobody else wanted.

I suppose he must also be crippled, retarded and blind, J. said, and his voice sounded gently amused. And kind.

My God, I thought, maybe he *does* know me. Maybe more than I know him.

I put my hand on his stomach (something I used to do) and I said no, I wasn't quite that demented. I said that I had been thinking about it (which I had not but it was as if I had thought it all out) and I wanted a child of 7 or 8 or 9. I figured I had about ten good years left and I could get such a child raised up before I fell apart.

You're sure it doesn't have to be crippled or paralyzed or deformed? he asked.

No. A perfectly normal child, I said. Just an older one. And of course he'd be black.

Of course, J. said, and he laughed.

Well, I said. Is that all right?

Let's think about it, he said. Let's think about it while we're off on that vacation.

What vacation, I started to say. Then I remembered

and I said, Oh, the island with Ames.

He asked would I mind if we didn't take Ames.

I said it was barely possible that I could stand it without her.

And he said that must mean I was feeling better about things because when he suggested taking her, he'd been sure I wouldn't go off anywhere alone with him. On account of your B.D. (he added). How is it, by the way?

I told him it did not seem to be terminal. Then I said, I am serious about adopting the child.

He said he was taking it seriously.

I said he'd better because I was going out, the first thing tomorrow morning, to an agency and get started on it. I was speculating aloud as to how long it would take and would there be any religious requirement and ruminating in general when I heard J.'s gentle snore.

This morning I got Mary Anne on the phone and she gave me all kinds of information on adoptions, where to go and how to proceed. She says there should be no trouble.

But you're crazy, she said. Do you realize all the problems such a child will have? What is this *for*, Sophie?

I said it was a child to comfort me in my old age.

You're crazy, she said again. Then she said, Well, if that's what you want, you won't have any trouble finding one. There are so many 7- or 8-year-old black children, you won't know which one to pick.

Oh, I'll know, I told her. I'll know the exact one when I see him. I have a picture of him in my mind's eye.

And I do. I will find him, and he will be ours. J.'s and mine. And Gabriel's and mine. And that great thing: himself.

ABOUT THE AUTHOR

Eliza McCormack was born and raised in North Carolina, where she still owns a 125-acre farm on which, she says, she raises nothing but a large crop of nostalgia.

She received a Ph.B. from the University of Chicago and a J.D. from the University of Chicago Law School. She practiced law for a time but gave it up because her legal briefs kept turning into short stories.

She now devotes herself to her writing and to her husband, with whom she lives in Cambridge, Massachusetts. Her favorite sport is scuba diving, which, she says, gives her the happy illusion that there is some hiding place down here.